The Sunbird

E.F. Fonkeng

Langaa Research & Publishing CIG
Mankon, Bamenda

Publisher
Langaa RPCIG
Langaa Research & Publishing Common Initiative Group
P.O. Box 902 Mankon
Bamenda
North West Region
Cameroon
Langaagrp@gmail.com
www.langaa-rpcig.net

Distributed in and outside N. America by African Books Collective
orders@africanbookscollective.com
www.africanbookcollective.com

ISBN: 9956-727-04-0

Dedication

To you, Scolastica
Who sped past Life,
Not even the Mountains
Bar the Memory
Of a sister

Chapter One

Mami Nawaya shook Scolastica violently, "Get up, my friend, do you see the time or do you not?"

The time, what time? As if her first night in this dwelling, she looked around and about her – in a bid to ascertain whether there was, indeed, a clock somewhere and anywhere.

She coiled and uncoiled her body like a snake and slid out of bed, groaning.

"And what is that nonsense?" her auntie inquired.

"Nothing, auntie."

"It better be."

She proceeded to the window, opened it and the full glare of the morning sun hit her in the face. Unusual, she thought, for this time of year – in fact, any time of year – for a town with a reputation of nothing but constant drizzle, fog, dampness and cold.

"Get away from there, you stupid thing," she shouted at a sunbird that had settled on a dress she had washed and dried outside but forget to bring in the night before. There were bird droppings glued all over the dress, thanks to the soft rain the night before. As far as she was concerned, this bird was the culprit. The little bird quickly dispatched on its way, Scolastica set about her morning chores - feed the pigs, sweep the compound inside-out, go fetch water from the local stream, among others. She was thankful it was not market day in Burwandai!

Throughout the day her mind kept looping back to the sunbird and its resilience before the elephant; it was one popular legend in these parts she had a hard time swallowing.

1

****

It was an incident that had drawn the instant and generalized ire of Burwandai's rumour mill. To its chief priestess, Mami Titi, it had the imprint of the nasty wizards and witches of Motombolombo all over it. And with it, Ekodinge's fortunes took a dramatic turn.

True, Ekodinge had been wrestling for many years. He was a good wrestler but nowhere near the town's favourite prodigy. In fact, on many occasions, he barely made the cut for the Burwandai youth team. No one in Burwandai could, therefore, truly declare having seen this day coming – a day that would come to be engraved in Scolastica's mind. How could Elempia have become the victim of such a freak trapping accident at this eleventh hour – just like that? A few accusing fingers were even pointed the way of Ekodinge's father, who doubled as coach of his town's squad. Not that any of this bothered Scolastica. In fact, upon getting wind of the news, she had run home, all full of excitement and broken it to her auntie. 'I see, and I wonder how that should concern us' was all auntie Nawaya had said, leaving Scolastica to ask herself how she could possibly be related to this woman - whose vital organs seemed to come to life only over insignificant matters. Meanwhile, try as hard as he did, not even Chief Nfombeng could get the *mukala* to postpone this annual festival to give Burwandai's favourite son time to heal. At stake was a trophy, the silver cup, and Burwandai would show up no matter what.

To the people of Burwandai - indeed, the entire Native Authority area, wrestling remained one of the few pleasures they had left, the *mukala* having suppressed and criminalized just about anything he fancied or that he, in his infinite wisdom, could not comprehend. Little wonder then that passions always rose to a pitch every time there was a *pala-pala* competition. And this one was no exception.

Having more than a passing interest in this particular wrestling competition, Scolastica had, with trepidation this time, joined the tens of supporters for the long trek to Motombolombo, the setting for this annual jamboree.

Upon arriving, they were met with an atmosphere that was casual, tense and exciting, all at once. The dresses, no, costumes were a rainbow kaleidoscope of colours that shone brightly under the hot afternoon sun. Motombolombo was bustling with more activity than usual as folks jostled to and from Pala-Pala Square and the myriad *mimbo* houses littered across this town. Even the palm and eucalyptus trees that surrounded the square seemed to be of the party atmosphere as their leaves and branches danced to the gentle rhythms of the cool breeze over this otherwise sleepy town. That is was all coming from the direction of the high and imposing Fongetafula, that served as a natural barrier between Motombolombo and Burwandai territory, was not unusual. To the folks of this entire region everything about the Fongetafula was wrapped in awe. Fongetafula, the home of Epasa Moto, half-human, half-deity, at whose feet they come, year in and year out, to lay their affliction of every persuasion, stoic in their belief in his mercy and blessing to vanquish even the most recalcitrant adversary, and more so on days like this one.

Every corner you turned in Pala-pala Square, the conversation was the same as excited groups of fans exchanged pleasantries followed by heated challenges, ultimately placing bets as to who would win *this* duel. Over the years, the duel had taken on the air of a rivalry between these two towns; they had met so many times in the finals – seven successive years – and it was a duel marked by a decidedly Motombolombo edge. But forget the past, at least, if you were Scolastica and her noisy bunch from Burwandai. As in the past, this duel comprised, in the main, young men who had just undergone their puberty rites. It was said, always in hushed tones, that the reason for this was to provide the *mukala* an opportunity to seek out young warrior types for his army and his many wars – and no one here could say why he was always fighting - in faraway lands. According to a matter-of-fact Mami Titi the *mukala* had also sent his excuses for missing this big one, having been summoned home by some woman they had made their chief for a silver cup trophy and a lot of cash to hand to the victor.

Meanwhile, back and forth went the bettors. After word had circulated that Motombolombo's famed wrestler, Teke Langamandu would be taking on some fellow from Burwandai named Ekodinge, Motombolombo fans became even more generous with their bet offers.

"I will give you this calabash and everything inside, plus five of my finest fowls should that your fellow you call a wrestler even win one round," declared the town's chief palm wine tapper to Ekodinge's father, who, fatigued from the long trek and all the pre-match excitement, was leaning against a tree. Like everyone else in the small Burwandai delegation he too must have been wondering how in the world the straws could have ended up this way, with his novice of a son as the final wrestler in a duel that had gone Motombolombo's way more often than he could remember or bother to recall.

"Where did the lazy fellows even learn how to wrestle?" another Motombolombo man jibed.

"Yes, someone asks that fellow to tell us where this *pala-pala* is taking place, eh," added a septuagenarian.

Ekodinge's father, it would seem, had been identified and singled out and now bore the brunt of the torrent of teases. It was as if this bunch was daring his son to put up any challenge! Scolastica, tired from cheering the spirits of Burwandai fans, with all that went into it, was taking a much deserved rest, sitting at a corner not far from Ekodinge's dad, in the company of two friends. They were munching on some home-made delicacies including *moy-moy* she had brought with her and listening to the verbal tirades being directed their way, her heart threatening to leap from inside her. Mboh Mutekah, fed up with the attacks, jolted to his feet and confronted the latest aggressor.

"We will show you today that all your past so-called victories have been as a result of *mungang*, which we shall uncover, trample upon and bury – right here!"

He remained on his feet.

"What is this shit that just came out of your mouth?" the chief palm wine tapper shot back.

"Forget fowls, I will give you my hunting gear – bow, arrow, powder, dog and even gun – should that your Mister Nobody manage to throw our son to the ground, even once."

He stomped his foot into the ground and drew several coffins, tombs for the yet-to-pass victim. He thumped his chest, licked his forefinger and raised it to the sky facing the Fongetafula, then spat on the ground - right in front of Mboh Mutekah. The back-and-forth betting was overshadowed only by the pulsating rhythms of the drums and the generalized frenzy. To which the dancers, which meant anyone fired up to jollificate, responded by stomping their feet and sending clouds into the air. The singing, of a melodious pitch, was led by some woman who, to Scolastica, looked like three rolled into one.

Suddenly, the singing, drumming, dancing, the bells, bets and threats that came with them all came to a halt. It was as if the sky was about to come out of place. The silence was interrupted only by a generalized shuffling of feet, raising of heads, shoving and jostling for position, the youngsters having taken the vantage viewing positions that the tree branches provided. Scolastica managed to force herself to the front of the ring, almost, rubbing, against her desire, her breasts against a multitude of people many of whom sent out a pungent smell of *kwacha* and *mimbo*, forcing her to cover her nostrils as she shuffled through. From the far distance could be heard the intermittent sound of the royal gong, horn and drums. That meant only thing: the presence, at this duel, of someone special; he was led into the square by a cortege comprising the gong-messenger, horn-blower, drummers, the palace griot, title-holders and the duo everyone had come to watch. The jubilation resumed as soon as this procession made its way into the square. The royal *mungang*, heavily multi-coloured, moved back and forth between the head and tail of the procession, his dark smoking pot dangling from one hip to the other. Two titled messengers helped their chief alight from his lion seat and gently placed him under a huge baobab at one end of the square on another seat carried in by a valet. To the ululations of the womenfolk. He was sure basking in the sunshine of his, by the incantations of the griot, glorious reign. No sooner was he installed than the *mungang* was at the centre of the court. He began to dance in circles, chanting incantations only he apparently understood. Just fine with the crowd. Even in Burwandai Scolastica had heard of cases where folks had been dragged before the dreaded and revered Obasinjom and fined for wondering aloud what business a *mungang* had showing up at a wrestling match. Then, with the speed unusual for a man his age, the *mungang* bolted from one end of the square to the other, each time dragging back with him a wrestler. Once in the centre of the court he made both wrestlers kneel and face the huge baobab. Scolastica was watching as if both eyes would fall off. So was Ekodinge's dad. Both wrestlers had their backs toward the great mountain of the gods behind which lay Burwandai country. The *mungang* dipped one hand into his smoking pot, poured some whitish-powdery stuff from a calabash unto his left palm. He rubbed the mixtures vigorously in between his palms and then proceeded to repeatedly scrub the chests of the wrestlers with a now clay-brown substance. Then he made them stoop, their hands on their knees, locking horns. It was now obvious he was going to double as the referee of this duel, and to that could be read glee on the faces of the Motombolombo folks and apprehension on those from Burwandai.

Teke Langamandu, the lion of Motombolombo, as he was fondly addressed by his admirers, was dressed in a loin wrapped in between his legs from the front to the back and tightly girded around the waist. He was tattooed – like a lion. Ekodinge too wore a loin the same manner as his rival. He was tattooed in the colour of the beast of the mighty Kekelekeh that ran close to Burwandai and inside which was said to reside all the *mungang* of the chiefdom. As if for emphasis, he had a crocodile-like tail hooked on to the rear end of his loin wrap.

The royal horn-blower blew into his horn. The *mungang*, who appeared to be relishing every moment of his prestidigitation, began:

"By the powers vested in me by his most powerful and ever generous, our beloved leader, Chief Lohkoh-Lohkoh here present, the personal representative of Epasa Moto and who rules in concert with and through our revered

Obasinjom, I now pronounce this season's *pala-pala* final on. And may it be the best the people of Motombolombo...and Burwandai have ever seen."

To the Burwandai fans it all sounded as if their town had been mentioned only as an after-thought. As he spoke, dark clouds descended upon the square from the direction of the imposing mountain.

"What is this, eh? What the hell did he spend all that time up Fongetafula for? And he calls himself *mungang? Mungang,* my foot!"

'This must be Motombolombo's version of Mami Titi,' thought Scolastica after she overheard the comments of some nearby folks about this woman. As she spoke, she was drowned by applause. Not many could tell exactly why but as much as could be deciphered through the thick clouds, it seemed as if Chief Lohkoh-Lohkoh had stood to give the traditional wave of the wand. The fight was on.

Both fighters charged forward at each other, to the frenetic beating of drums, the ululations of the women and cheering from the crowd. The clouds were receding just as quickly as they had formed. Scolastica, feeling a rush of hot blood inside her, felt like diving into the ring to wrestle her man from the pangs of the lion and put a stop to all this nonsense. First, it was the first-time finalist from Burwandai, who grabbed his opponent by the torso with his left hand, and with the right, pulled him forward by the neck. A simultaneous right foot tackle brought Teke Langamandu down on his back. Scolastica and the Burwandai supporters, diligently keeping to their corner, erupted with glee. A second tussle produced a similar result! It was obvious what Ekodinge lacked in masculinity he sure made up for in agility. Many Motombolombo fans simply slapped the air, the head palm wine tapper and running commentator conveying their collective feeling.

"Small pickin cutlass di sharp for morning time," he declared.

Maybe it was, as he said, the case of the novice who, always sharp and first off the blocks, was never anywhere to be seen by the end of a task. But no one among these diehards – on either side – could tell, for certain. After all, did the people not also live by the code that gave to time everything? As the man spoke, their veteran, in one swift move, pulled Ekodinge forward with the right hand, using the left forearm as a shield into which Ekodinge banged himself. And before he could regain his balance, Teke Lagamandu pinned his right foot to the ground, right behind Ekodinge toward which he flung him. Back to the ground! A stylish win, indeed.

"What did I tell all you doubters, eh?" cried the commentator as the drumming, the singing, the ululations, and with them the wriggling of buttocks of different shapes and sizes, all rose to a crescendo. A true feast for the eyes!

On and on wrestled the fighters, with none giving in to the agile and cunning moves of the other. The sun, which has resurfaced for a while, was again going to sleep behind the Fongetafula and still no winner had emerged. But the epic was only entering its climax. Strange indeed that their man was still in this thing, the Burwandai fans were scratching their heads, questioning their hearts and yes, holding their collective breath.

"Three straight strikes from one and it's over," intoned the *mungang* at the end of a long break he had given the visibly exhausted wrestlers. It was a break well spent for the bettors and supporters of both fighters who each carried their man around the square, chanting, waving leaves and anything else that could be waved, teasing, all in an obvious attempt to intimidate the opposite camp. When the tussle resumed the duo charged at each other with such ferocity they knocked the *mungang* to the grass - to the chuckles of many. This time it was the short and stocky veteran of Motombolombo who caught Ekodinge on one thigh; so firm was the grip that the crocodile actually let out a loud cry. But somehow he managed to land on his buttocks as the lion pushed him backward with tremendous vigour before pouncing for the finish. The crocodile slipped, just a little, to one side as the lion's head slid through into a circle Ekodinge had made with his right arm. Then, swiftly, he swung the rest of his body to the right, toward Teke Langamandu, whose head was still firmly in his grip. Back to the ground! The next bout produced another win for the lanky crocodile man. By this time the crowd was near dead; even their drums seemed to play with less intensity as concern could be read on their faces. It seemed an eternity before the combatants engaged in the penultimate round. As if he had read the writing on the wall, Motombolombo's man did not even put up a fight worth the name; it was over in a flash with the lion's back flat on the ground. Burwandai fans suddenly exploded into wild ecstasy, burst into the centre of the square, hoisted their man high up to the gods and commenced the dancing victory parade. Scolastica was jumping, screaming and crying with joy, wanting nothing more in the world at this moment than to wrestle him from those multiple hands hoisting him out of her reach, fling herself at him, drag them both to the earth and rain kisses on him, and yes, let herself be totally devoured by her champion crocodile. Oh yes, as far she was concerned, he was now hers. For now, she had to contend herself with being part of the boisterous hand-clappers, singers and dancers. As if by some magic, the crowd started to alternate between shouts of 'Ekodinge' and 'Scolastica.' It was a clear invitation to the one whose moniker was 'the-one-who-sings-like-a-bird' to lead them in a parade all the way back to Burwandai.

Chapter Two

Ekodinge's championship win was like the okro soup he had been waiting for to eat his bowl of *fufu*. Scolastica opened up to him in more ways than one.

They had been growing up in Burwandai together now for some time. She was a beautiful, a bit flirtatious but by no means wayward teenager living with her aunt. He lived with his parents. They were genuinely attracted to each other; to the town's rumour mill and Auntie Nawaya, once she got to know about it, that was tantamount to having an affair. She vehemently disapproved of it. It did not occur to her – or she chose to ignore – the fact that she had played a huge role in stoking and fanning the flame of this fire she so desperately was now fighting to put out. To her and her family – or so she maintained – Ekodinge was a wretched young man with no future, and not even his *pala-pala* championship win could change that. And the woman let him know this at every opportunity she got. Still, Scolastica would not keep away from Ekodinge, not even after her aunt made it known to her one of the town's prosperous businessmen was interested in her. Auntie Nawaya tried every trick in the book to fire up an interest for Zhondezi in her.

Returning from market one late afternoon, she spotted Scolastica and Ekodinge in an uncompromising position; the one had the hand clasped into that of the other. It was an opportunity for a mother-to-daughter talk later that evening. Scolastica's buttocks had barely made contact with the kitchen stool than Mami Nawaya began, navigating between scolds, invocations and even pleadings

"I want to let you know I saw you with that good-for-nothing today," she began ominously.

"And you dared to follow him all the way to I don't – know-where! You thought I would not know, right? You capital fool! You take me for a fool, right?"

She put her hands on her head and exclaimed, "My ancestors, what harm did I commit to deserve this?"

When Scolastica did not say anything, she continued, "My friend, am I not talking to you?"

'But you never thought about that when you were sending me there every day,' she murmured.

"What was that?" her auntie inquired.

"Nothing auntie, nothing." She sounded angry, which seemed to have touched her auntie's soft spot; she brought down her fire a notch.

"Look, all you have to do is say yes to my rich and handsome in-law and you will never have to live the type of rake-and-scrape life your poor auntie is living," Or do you too want to suffer the way I am?"

Rich, maybe, but calling this fellow handsome was the mother of all understatements, thought Scolastica, who countered, "But auntie, he is old enough to be my father."

"And what does it matter? I say it is all in your little head. Age, age, age, nonsense. Tell me, can you put youth in the pot and eat plantains with?"

"But he already has two other wives."

"Yes? Your auntie was a co-wife, I guess it is some curse for which we must now seek the mercy of Epasa Moto? I say curse, ten-fold, to those who are putting this poison into that skull of yours. Or, don't you realize that as the newest and youngest wife you will instantly become and, I bet you, remain the apple of his heart and attention?"

"Auntie, Ekodinge and I love ourselves and we need your blessing."

"Yes, and after that we shall all be eating love, wearing love and asking love to treat us when we fall sick."

Then, the preacher in her took over. "I will let you understand that this your love is not some wondrous wonder never before seen or experienced. It is nothing but one side of the palm, the other side of which is marriage. I mean, what our people hold to be true of marriage is equally true of love; it is not a meal prepared."

Scolastica was staring at her with scorn but she could care less.

"Like a garden, love can grow, if we tender to it," she concluded.

Scolastica, in part because she made absolutely no sense from what she had just heard, tried to switch the topic.

"But, auntie, you keep saying that he has no future, don't you know that since he won the wrestling championship, Chief Nfombeng has bestowed on his father another feather on his titled cap, and has made Ekodinge a special messenger for his council?"

"Ekodinge, special messenger for the chief," she mimicked. And then her voice was up again.

"Foolish girl, you hear me? I say you are a very foolish girl. Instead of going after something that will bring honour to your family, you want to rub the name of this proud family into the mud."

"But auntie..."

"Oh, stop, I don't want to hear anymore. Auntie, auntie..."

There was a knock on the door. Scolastica saw an opportunity and jumped to her feet.

"Sit," she ordered.

"But I always answer the door, when..."

"I will get it," she answered tersely. Odd, thought Scolastica. As she stood, she turned around, looked at Scolastica piercingly and added, "Pay attention to that pot on the fire, my friend. And we are not over with this, not by a long shot."

With that, she bolted out of the kitchen. All Scolastica could hear was the exchange of greetings; it all sounded friendly.

"Massa has sent me to give you this small bundle," a male voice said. "That to tell you he has just returned from his journey but that he will be around for only three days before getting on the road again."

"Thank, no greet him for me. I will come thank him, myself," her auntie replied.

It was obvious every objection, however spirited, that Scolastica was mounting continued to be neutralized by the sin of Zhondezi's largesse toward her auntie.

It was now several months after Ekodinge's wrestling victory, and try as they could to have it otherwise, the two were now being seen together more often than before. However, they seemed not to be discrete enough, even as Scolastica, especially, continued to put in a lot of effort at countering auntie Nawaya's plan.

It was a cool night. The high moon, like a clumsy woman pounding *fufu* and with a baby on her back, shone brightly in the sky. The crickets were out in force, so were the children, singing and dancing to the *mbolo-mbolo,* the ultimate night-time game of the truancies of young love. The pair stood under a mango tree, hands, feet and lips clasped into one another. They were watching the silhouettes of the children.

"How long have we been special friends?" she began.

"I don't know, ever since I won the championship?" he ventured.

"Three years, you liar."

"What three years?"

"Are you sure you have not had your mind on me since the first day you saw me?"

"You call that special friendship? And are sure you too have not had your eyes on me since then? Always coming to our house pretending to have a message for my mother..."

"I say, liar," as she brushed his cheek with a gentle slap. Then, her tone changed. "I need you to promise me something."

"What is it?"

"You promise you will not get angry at what I am about to tell you?"

"Well, tell me first, then, I can say whether I will be angry or not."

"What a cunning fellow."

"Remember, it is cunning that won me the championship."

"I get it, he has won one match, I bet I will no longer have peace in this town as a result."

"Point of correction, won not just a match but the championship." He was enjoying himself.

"Do you love me?" she shot out.

"Love, that is a troublesome question, you know.. And a bit silly at that, if you ask me."

"Really? Silly, eh?" She punched him.

"Ouch! No, I did not mean it that way."

"Now, will you stop playing defensive and answer the damn question?"

"And the question is...?"

"Oh my God, Ekodi! Now, seriously, does Ekodi love Scolastica?"

"Yes, I do and I promise to..."

"You promise to what?"

"Whatever comes after."

"Then lick your tongue! I say lick your tongue to prove it," she ordered.

"Come on, you know that is impossible."

Love, always taking liberties, was in full display here, and Ekodinge noticed it.

"But whatever I do, you can't see."

"I say do it." And before he could react she poured on the onslaught, "Eh, what is this infidelity I sense on the part of my man?"

Ekodinge remained silent but gave her one long caustic look. Not that she noticed it. She, on her part, savoured every moment of her victory. When it came to the game of mental gymnastics she was in a league of her own.

"I need you to promise me one thing," she continued, as she squeezed her body even harder against his. Ekodinge feeling the full force of his young manhood piercing through his quarter-to-long and her nipples against his chest, answered, rather feebly, "what?"

"Ah ah, promise first, know after."

"I promise."

"To stand by your woman in the face of even a volcanic eruption from the Fongetafula?"

I said "I promise," he added, losing his willpower.

"I am pregnant."

Ekodinge tore himself off her grip, jerked backwards and pushed her backwards on the shoulder all at once.

"Who?"

She charged at him.

"What a stupid question, who else?"

He interrupted the long silence that ensued with "Does she know about this?"

"Ah, your house is on fire and you are chasing a fleeing rat? Is that it, Ekodi?"

"And if you are referring to my auntie, not yet."

"Fine."

"She is bound to know, some time, you know. And why do you say 'fine'?"

"Honestly, I don't know."

They had managed, before separating for the night, to arrive at a truce and to mutually convince themselves that everything was going to be alright. Through it all she had wanted but could not bring herself to telling him how she had been hoping being heavy with child for him would make it impossible for her family to sell her off to some fellow twice her age.

'Spirits of my ancestors, don't tell me she could have planned this.' He was talking to himself as he made his way home. And did it really matter now? What if it backfired? He whacked himself on the head. Neither of them had any sleep that night.

****

The woman who had all her tentacles on the plough, it seemed, got to know about the pregnancy sooner than its architects had wished. She seemed to be ever ready – for anything, and not even Scolastica's pregnancy would shake her determination. Once she became aware of it, she who, if one asked Scolastica, had enjoyed her unfair share of Zhondezi's largesse, swung into action, again, sooner than its authors had time to come up with any other strategy. Ekodinge was weaving a *kenja* when Scolastica dashed in to narrate, amid tears, the latest.

"That you-know-who must not see us together," Ekodinge said as soon as he saw her approaching. He let out his hand, which she took, and led her inside, to his room. She did not wait for him to ask.

"Ekodi, she knows."

It was always sweet music to his ears when she called him this way. But there was nothing sweet about this moment.

"Is that why you are crying? Come on, wipe your eyes. What exactly does she know?" He was merely trying to reassure himself.

"Everything."

"And how did she find out?"

"The female examination, does it matter?"

"So, she was bound to find out, some time, don't you think?"

"There is more, worse!" Ekodinge readjusted his buttocks on the bed. Even the elephant grass that made up the contents of his mattress seemed, for the first time, to be pricking him on the buttocks.

"She is shipping me off to Kikaikilaiki."

"Kikai- what? How come? When?" He took Scolastica's hands into his, squeezed them and held on to them. When he noticed she hesitated on which response to give first, he re-phrased his question, "When?"

"If you mean when I am going, she did not say but, from the seriousness with which she said it, it cannot be long from now. She just kept repeating something like 'he must not know about this, no, he must not know about this.'"

"Him meaning whom, and know what?"

"How would I know? Are we in court, Ekodi?"

"Sorry, and oops... but, seriously, when did she tell you this?"

"She announced it last week."

"Yeah?, announced – since last week and you did not tell me until now?"

"It's not like there is anything anyone can do to stop this, is there? Besides, you know how difficult it is becoming these days for us to meet. She has spies all over the place."

"It's not her, it's that you-know-who."

They remained silent, absorbing each other's pain, for a long time. Then, Scolastica broke it, "Kikaikilaika, that's it, she announced – just like that! And this when we were deep into preparing *timba-mbusa*, Ekodi. Do you know what that means?"

He was speechless.

"That means the breaking of an unbreakable bond. Isn't that what *timba-mbusa* means?"

"Did she say she was doing this to break up something?"

"She said something like 'not when I still have some breath in me will I let this shame and calamity happen to the proud line of Bandialare.'"

"So, I am now shame and calamity, Ekodi?"

"Please, Scola, stop. You are no calamity, let alone shame." He was going along with the motions, not quite sure of what he could do to help.

She went on to narrate how her auntie said she had received a message from Tobeningo and that this was the collective decision of the family; how she Scolastica had no intention of calling her a liar, but how she knew better who in this family held the yam and the knife. Did her own father, younger to this auntie by a couple of births, not always address her *'mami'*? And how could a son dare to challenge his mother?

She unveiled to Ekodinge the details of the plan that would guide and rule over her life for the next several years, as revealed to her by her auntie.

To both, as they sat there, reflecting, Kikaikilaiki could well have been on another planet. It was at least three days of torture away from Burwandai, much of it on foot and, if one were lucky, in what folks here had, not without a pinch of humour, baptized *spana-nkononi*.

The relationship between the two locales was not the most cordial, even. They both recalled at least one war between the two localities in the not-too-distant past. One incident in particular remained glued to Scolastica's memory. The women of Burwandai had, one cold morning, marched to the office of the *mukala* and bared their womanhood over something. The war had ended with the victory of Kikaikilaiki - so said the *mukala*, who had then proceeded to impose a punishing levy on every Burwandai man, woman, child and even property, it seemed. And here she was being slammed into a slammer deep inside enemy territory!

"As if this were not enough, there is never, I mean never any news and gossip between that place and here," Ekodinge lamented.

The burden of her fate soon tired her out and she fell asleep in Ekodinge's arms. No sooner had she dozed off than she was again visited by the saga.

'Look at it this way, my dear,' her auntie was telling her, 'here, you will be able to give birth in complete privacy, away from all those gossip mills, and before you know it, you will be a hot commodity again for any man to sweep you off your feet.' She felt her heart leap from its place. 'Maybe this woman will let me marry the man of my dreams, after all. But then, the witch – the spirits bless her for thinking this way of her aunt – turned right back to stirring her brew, as usual. 'The family has unanimously agreed it will spill the beans on you should you turn down their choice of a husband. That way, you can kiss marriage goodbye for good.'

'Me, not to have a husband, and become the laughing stock of the land among my mates? No way!'

She had managed to sound defiant but she could feel every bone in her breaking into pieces. And to think that all of this was happening to her within the first week of her arrival. If she did not die here, she resolved, she would come out a much stronger woman.

It was getting dark outside when Ekodinge woke her from her slumber.

"Oh, I guess I was dreaming."

"My dear, I think I should take you home before your auntie raises hell." He kissed her on the cheek.

****

Her stay in Kikaikilaiki was uneventful. Her hopes for an elaborate and exciting *ekekweh* had been dashed the day she set foot in town. Oh well, by her pregnancy – if truth be told. The prime reason for *ekekweh* was to advertise the maidens of marriageable age, who had been extensively and privately groomed in the etiquettes of marriage, to prospective husbands. Even if after giving birth she decided to fake it? Her auntie was again thinking for her.

"I am sorry, my dear, but we cannot organize one for you," Auntie Dominica had declared in a matter-of-fact manner. "While I cherish it, the outing ceremony for the *ekekweh* also comes with lots of these gossip-types; even the road to Burwandai could suddenly develop ears."

'Birds of a feather sure flock together,' was all that came to her mind when this other auntie finished.

****

While she laboured in her secret prison Ekodinge had no clue over what was actually going on. He was bound to the dictates of this woman; Mami Nawaya, with not much room to manoeuvre. At least, that is what his friend Jenje Moto kept repeating to him. Not as if he had not realized it by himself!

Nor was he indifferent to the many rumours going around town: this woman was a *mami wata*, who, every now and then at night transformed into an elephant to go destroy the farm of any one who dared to pick a quarrel with her. After all, why did she not have any children of her own but for the fact that she had sold her womb in exchange for her elephant powers. He could not dare to offend her. Shortly after Scolastica's departure from Burwandai Ekodinge approached Mami Nawaya.

"And to what do I owe this unwanted visit?" she inquired as soon as she saw him entering the yard.

"Auntie, I have..."

"Hold it right there, fellow," she cut him short. "Who do you call auntie? If you don't have anything better to say, I suggest you turn right around and ask your feet to lead you back to where they brought you from."

"But I come in peace and not war, if you will only hear me out."

Mami Nawaya just stood there, at akimbo, starring at the motion picture.

"How is Scolastica?"

"Scola, who? Look my friend, if you have been sent I suggest you go tell whoever has sent you that you did not see me."

"All I ask for is to know how she is doing and if I can be of any help." He pretended not to know where she was.

"You are still standing there?"

24

She disappeared indoors. The next thing Ekodinge saw was a pot of hot water being hurled his way. He waited past another market day for her temper to cool off. And when a third visit resulted in the woman chasing him off with a cutlass, Ekodinge got the message; he would look for other ways to get in touch with the love of his life than expose life and limb to such grave danger. Nawaya, they called this woman - that sounded indeed like war.

Zhondezi, for his part, got nothing but one twisted tale after the other about his wife-to-be. Both aunts worked extra hard to always sugar-coat their tales, largely in response to the sway the man's deep purse held over their lives. Scolastica was undergoing *ekekweh*; it was taboo to see a woman in these condition, environment and period; a man of his calibre required a woman who was well-groomed – it was a deep trough from which they fished.

Throughout her stay in Kikaikilaiki, Ekodinge did not manage to get a single message to Scolastica. It was as if Mami Nawaya was watching the hawk's every move even in the absence of the chick. By the time she gave birth her family had arranged for her return to her father's compound in Tobeningo in expectation of the arrival of Zhondezi for the formal marriage rites. Barely a week before her scheduled departure her auntie landed the bombshell.

"My dear, I hope you are not unaware of the impossibility of taking the baby along with you."

'Auntie Dominica, I don't understand."

"What is there not to understand, my daughter? At times like these even the leaves of the trees have been known to have ears. Your husband might have his people on the ground; they may spot you, I mean, the baby, and you can't pretend to not know what that would mean to you and your future, do you?"

It was a statement, not a question, and it was clear from her every mannerism and the way she picked her words that she had put a lot of thought into this. This one had always been far less abrasive than her sister at Burwandai but no less authoritarian.

As Scolastica continued to listen, looking perplexed, her aunt added, "Your auntie in Burwandai and I have made all the necessary arrangements for the baby to be well looked after – right here. You can always come to visit, anytime." Then, she threw in the now-familiar line; it was the decision of the family. And with that she put the final seal on the coffin. Even the night creatures were all going to sleep, but that night, Scolastica would not sleep, as she sobbed like never before in her life. She was convinced this punishment would never be meted out to her had her mother been alive.

Chapter Three

Mami Nawaya sat on a bamboo stool in the shade of an orange tree in her yard. The sun, strange for this locale, albeit even in the dry season, was in full circle and undisturbed by any shade whatsoever. She was taking in every bit of the moment as she peeled beans she had left to soak and soften overnight.

Time could have sauntered but none of her mistrust and disdain for Ekodinge. It did not help matters the fact that Ekodinge's fortunes had not undergone any significant improvement over the same period. He showed up at Mami Nawaya's that afternoon determined, as usual. Uppermost in his mind was the question of the child. It was sometime now since he had come up with a new strategy, but he resolved that at any time during their argument, and as soon as he saw the woman disappear into the house or any enclosed surrounding he too would immediately disappear before calamity struck. The woman did not allow him to string even two sentences together.

"My child, did you say? With whom, and who told you that?"

"She told me she was pregnant for..."

"Shhh, keep your tongue back in its place, my friend. You want to put out my burning candle? I swear by the spirits of my ancestors it will be an all-out war between us if you do. And you know what happens in a war, don't you?"

"I do not seek to make war with you. I seek only to raise my son or daughter the way any loving father would want to."

"And what makes you think she kept it, or that you are the father?"

"The spirits of our ancestors forbid! Auntie, how can you even say such a thing?"

"Your ancestors, not mine. You think all it takes to be a father is to get a woman pregnant? Anyway, she did not tell me her destination, okay? And I warn you, cease bugging me."

"Please, just tell me where they are, I beg you. I miss them very much."

"I bet you have wax in those rabbit ears of yours. Or do you think I am deceiving you? I have no cause to, but I'd be damned if I let you or anyone get away with a calabash of palm oil where he did not harvest nor cook the palm bunches."

"I want to make amends, auntie."

"I said I am not your auntie." Then, she mimicked, 'I want to make amends, auntie.' "Can you? I say can you compensate me for all these years of the hard work you were supposed to be doing? Well, start talking - and doing. I am all ears - and watching."

The days gave room to weeks and months and the routine remained unchanged: appeals and the infrequent mild threat back and forth.

Then just like that she began to accept favours from Ekodinge and to have him perform one chore after another. Most of the gifts were for Scolastica, she continued to insist, and would duly be forwarded to her. She still would not confirm whether she was with child or not.

Ekodinge could only guess this shift in disposition had occurred in spite of her – and not in spite of him, somehow. It all occurred within a few moon cycles. In a rare fit of bravado he had transformed what would otherwise have been a shouting match between them into a high-stakes-game-of-cards. That evening, even his friend had remarked that, for

28

one who hardly drank, he had had a little too much *kwacha*, which he topped with a shot of the all too potent local whiskey, *kai-kai*. Then, he had marched to Nawaya's and announced, "I will tell whoever shows up to marry your daughter that she already has a child with another man, that you know about it and are hiding it from him." The old woman had stood transfixed and speechless for a while before resuming her usual combative spirit.

"You will do no such thing, fellow. You seem to naively underrate the fury of an old lady. I will finish you before you even begin and not even Epasa Moto up there on the Fongetafula will be able to stop me." Then, she continued, "I will tell whoever, na, na, na. What makes you think you will not be walking into a trap with both feet? And to think that all these years I have been the one restraining my son-in-law from consulting Obasinjom on you, or even worse."

"Consulting Obasinjom, on?" Ekodinge had asked meekly, unsure of the sudden change of the card in his hand. He had gone home that night feeling both elated at his act of braveness but also terrified at what would happen next.

Not much exchange of anything took place between him and old Nawaya for a while after the incident. But when it resumed, the old woman was a whole new and strange creature. They both preferred to let sleeping dogs lie as he continued to be a model helper – or prisoner – of hers, all the while with his eyes over his shoulders.

Then, on one market day it happened. It was the last market day before the big Kwanzaa celebration. Everyone in Burwandai, it seemed, was in a shopping frenzy, selling or buying something – or both. The market was overflowing with folks from far and near. This market day also happened to coincide with what the folks referred to simply as Banana Day. It was the day farmers – and around here that meant almost every adult male – received pay for their banana crop harvest and sale. Folks were treating themselves to their heart's desire, stocking up for Kwanzaa, and also paying their accumulated debts. A day like this, it was well-known over here, often heralded many a sweet and sour love story.

Zhondezi had gone to Tobeningo to sell his wares. He always maintained that Tobeningo folks were not only richer but were also more open to displaying their wealth. He would also use the opportunity to celebrate Kwanzaa with his wife Scolastica.

Not even the presence of Massa Mukwata could dampen the spirit of this day. The head banana inspector was loathed like no other, more so in Burwandai than any other place in the entire Native Authority area. His crime: deliberately – from the perspective of the people of this town – downgrading the quality of their banana harvests with what amounted to a sadistic passion. No, not even the diminutive, stocky specimen of a human being, installed at Mami Kwacha and tanking *kwacha* and palm wine with reckless abandon, could keep away from nor punctuate the generalized gaiety of the moment. It was not long before the little boys and girls spotted him, and, like flies before a carcass, they at once assembled around Mami Kwacha, spewing out in song, as always, one hostile satire after another. For, even these children, little yet cruel in their own way, were not innocent of the fact that this man stood between them and that nice and special dress and meal for the Kwanzaa season. In the midst of the generalized melee Nawaya spotted Ekodinge. Their eyes met and she beckoned him far away from her stand and from the purview of those prying Burwandai ears and eyes, many among them with gaping mouths, to boot.

"I'd like to see you after market, when the sun goes down. And don't fail, neither should you be late."

Ekodinge's head was turning on itself as he headed out of the market square to go find his friend.

"My brother, I tell you, it is true what they say about market day in these parts," he began as soon as he caught up with Jenje Moto.

"That we should not work up a sweat if Epasa Moto himself showed up on a market day," his friend finished his thought for him.

"Ah, you are so right on that one, foolish man."

They sat on the trunk of a felled mango tree in his yard and together began to extol the virtues - no, the omnipotence - of market day in Burwandai, wondering if any other place on earth saw so much activity, so much strangeness and surprises as Burwandai on market day. Did one expression, common on the lips of people here, not capture it all? It's market day, I can expedite your journey to your ancestors – and pay the fine! Then, he brought up the invitation offer from Nawaya.

"What do you think, should I go?"

"Any apprehension? After all, what is the worst that could happen? The woman drops some kind of fly of a portion in your soup..."

Ekodinge gave his friend one dirty look.

"I am sorry, I should know better than to clown over such a serious matter as love. Yes, you are in love and so, you will honour that invitation for the sake of love. Or, are you now out of love?"

Ekodinge was staring at him, almost in disbelief, as he added, "I am serious, for how else will you get to find out about Scola?"

These two were like the tongue and the mouth, and so as soon as his friend made the pronouncement, Ekodinge jumped to his feet, took leave of his friend, rushed indoors, had a rubdown, put on a tacky pair of trousers the image of a cock all over it and headed off to his meeting with Mami Nawaya.

****

"I prepared your favourite," she announced as soon as he walked in through the door and sat down. The mahogany – or was it iroko – furniture was still exhibiting a shiny glow of kerosene and palm oil polish it just received for the upcoming Kwanzaa.

"Good evening auntie, and what is my favourite, if I may ask?"

"You think I don't know? *Timba-mbusa*, of course."

"And to what do I owe this royal treatment?"

"Ah ah, do we need any other reason to celebrate than the fact that it is Kwanzaa? Time to thank the spirits for all our blessings, time to wish for a good harvest next season, for all good things, and time to forgive our enemies." It was a rambling even she seemed to get lost in.

"And I suppose I come in here as enemy?"

She ignored the question.

Laughing, she disappeared into the kitchen. When she returned, she had in her hands a large tray of *timba-mbusa* drenched in seasoned palm sauce with huge chunks of stock fish sprinkled liberally all over. Next, she brought a calabash of corn beer. She placed everything on a small centre table and covered the contents with *tima-casa*, a rainbow-coloured cloth reserved only for august occasions.

"I made this just for you."

Times like this recalled, once more, the high and esteemed faith that was roundly placed on this dish as the reconciler, anytime and anywhere, of a troubled relationship, even one in tatters. Very apt, Ekodinge thought, the song the people had and sang about this dish:

Ah, timba-mbusa,
No matter where I go
I will return for you
No matter where you run to,
My love, you will be back,
Even if I have to bring you, myself

Well, forget the song; for now, Ekodinge had in front of him the real deal. He washed his hands and delved into it.

"You prepared this for the enemy," teased Ekodinge, his mouth loaded and halfway through his meal. "Seriously, there must be a reason for you inviting me here this evening."

"Now that you asked, I want you to know that I have not been deaf to your appeals to have your son handed to you. But it won't be overnight as you have to give me more time to convince my family on your behalf. I hope you understand."

"Did you say a son? Oh spirits of Epasa Moto, I salute you," he smiled, going down on his knees and lifting both arms into the air.

"You will swear before our ancestors to keep this between you and I - and the spirits - for now. and you know the wrath of the spirits should you go contrary to what you swear before them"

"Oh auntie, I will, I do so swear! A son to continue my line, ah."

He had a million questions but none of that seemed to matter now as he simply let the rivulet of tears flow freely down his cheeks and unto his shirt and chest. Overcome with emotion, he had not been able to continue with his meal, as the conversation focused on the nitty-gritty of how he would eventually reunite with his son.

The relationship between the two remained cordial after this; it was due more to Ekodinge's scrupulous respect of the terms than on some angelic transformation on the part of Scolastica's aunt. In fact, so committed to the scheme was Ekodinge that he, on many occasions, went beyond the call of duty.

"Any default and this whole thing blows up in our faces," she had warned for the umpteenth time before going on to repeat how it had cost her to convince Scolastica's dad and the family to agree to the possibility of turning over the child to its father.

It was like another eternity waiting for the day when this woman and whoever was with her in this scheme would decide, from the goodness of their heart, that, yes, he had been punished enough to warrant some penance.

One of the things Ekodinge swore to was not to attempt to contact Scolastica nor send her any presents directly. He did not dare tell her he had twice before tried to get in touch with Scolastica through some Awarawa traders. These people were reputed to possess the singular capacity to reach anywhere they could make some money. Indeed, it was common knowledge around town – not that anyone could confirm nor deny – that their kind inhabited every corner of the planet. Unfortunately for him, Scolastica's aunt seemed to have her ears to the ground everywhere. She had consequently made him understand she was aware of his investigations and had warned him of the consequences if he persisted.

He was not much into any particular view of the cosmos. But as he walked home late that night he could not help but wonder if Nawaya had not suddenly realized how close she was to joining her ancestors. It was not uncommon for such individuals to suddenly begin to let go of the little things of this earth to focus instead on the big picture, that of working to secure for themselves a soft seat among their ancestors. Whatever it was, the news was too good to keep to himself and the evening too sweet and suddenly still too young to end now. He was singing to himself and with the tiny creatures of the night as he switched course and headed to Jenje Moto's.

Chapter Four

His son was brought and dropped off at his place with as little pomp as possible. It was even luck that had him at home when the old woman and her entourage of two showed up unannounced. Not the best of timing for either side. Ekodinge had all along assumed and expected that he would be given some kind of advance notice on this momentous day. Here he was scrambling to even ensure a befitting welcome reception for his guests. Worse, he had not yet prepared his newly arrived and pregnant bride to the fact that he was already a father to a big boy. It was a curious and uncomfortable first several minutes as both sides just stood there, face to face, not saying anything that made any sense. So awkward was the moment that Ekodinge could overhear a member of the less-than-august party ask Nawaya is she was sure they had entered the right compound. Most perplexed was Ekodinge's wife, hands at akimbo and transfixed to the spot with sweat down her armpits and unto the rim of her *kabba* on this otherwise cool afternoon.

"Oh please, do come in," Ekodinge announced, finally.

"Excuse my manners," apologized his wife, forcing a clean pair of teeth and frantically wiping each seat with the bottom and overflowing end of her *kabba* before it made contact with each occupant's buttocks.

The party was hardly seated than Ekodinge, beaming with delight, focused his gaze on the little boy, and spoke, "And who do we have here?"

The little boy turned and looked at his mother's aunt as if to ascertain from her what to say.

"Your papa," she said, shifting gazes from father to son and back to father again. Ekodinge briefly raised his head as he squatted to be on a face-to-face level with his son. He turned his head around as his eyes met with his wife's who forced a smile and quickly disappeared into the kitchen, a pot in her hand. He quickly focused his attention back on his son who gingerly walked into his open embrace. He tapped the child thrice on the back and held on to him until he was forced to let go to wipe his misty eyes. The child walked back to his mom's aunt's corner just as Ekodinge walked up and whispered something into her ear. She got up and followed him outside, assuring the little boy, "Sit here, grandma is coming."

They were hardly out of the house when Ekodinge almost thundered, "But auntie, why didn't you tell me you were coming?"

"I thought you were dying to see your son?"

"I could have made sure to organize a reception for you, one befitting of the occasion."

Silence.

"You know that's not the point. It's your wife, isn't it?" She was staring right into his eyes.

"Gosh, how can you say that?" "Didn't you see how happy she is?"

"Looking at this head, can you count the amount of grey hair on it?"

Silence from Ekondinge.

"Well, if you can't then you also can't fool me, young man. I was not born yesterday."

Still not a word from Ekodinge.

"So, you want me to take him back?"

Now, he shot back, "What are you talking? Truly, I don't understand you." "Gosh, I could have prepared her than to have this kind of surprise sprung on her."

"So, it is your wife, after all. You made my life a living hell because of your son. Now, I have brought him and all you can do is stand here shaking like dry banana leaves in the wind and mouthing about your wife. You expect me to solve all your family problems, mister. Now, go in there and start behaving like someone with something between his legs, and don't waste my time."

Who said a leopard could ever change its spots, thought Ekodi, as the woman simply brushed him aside and started to make it back into the house. A few steps away, she swung around and ordered, "My guests and I are hungry and thirsty." With that, the lion-woman disappeared inside, a perplexed Ekodinge not far behind.

The heavy feasting went on late into the night; many had simply dropped by out of curiosity. He had scurried around Burwandai to borrow a cock and corn beer here, several jugs of *kwacha* and some *kai-kai* there to satisfy the demands of the moment. There was also a bag of rice, a bunch of plantains and much more. He would spend the next year paying off the debts of this night of reunion. For now, he had a new lease of life. He wondered if it was true what they said and the code they seemed to live by here - that one never marries the woman one loves because of love's knack of flying out the window once the trap has caught its prey. What that had to do with this moment, he could not exactly figure out. He was not even certain over the accuracy of his thought.

Chapter Five

Scolastica returned to her father's compound still nursing the hope of seeing Ekodinge again. Even as she stared hopelessness in the face she was hatching a plan of her own. It was not clear even to her the contour, if any, of such a plan; still, she nursed it. Meanwhile, true to the plan her aunt had laid out, Zhondezi had showed up in Tobeningo shortly after her return. The marriage concluded and consummated in a whole week of fanfare, her husband had presented her with an offer that shocked, amazed and thrilled her all at the same time.

It was the night before they were to return to Burwandai. In one of her moments of inattention, he caught her by the waist, gently pulling on the elaborate rings of expensive and ornamented beads he had got for her as a wedding gift. The beads were generously spread all over her ankles, wrists, forearms, neck and hips, a feast for eyes and a statement to the weight of the man who had taken her for a wife. Without much emotion on her face or body, she obliged, laying her back on his hairy chest. Still heavy with the punchy smell of palm wine, *kwacha* and Panya wine combined, Zhondezi allowed the fingers of both arms to fiddle their way into her loosely strewn blouse and unto the nipples of her heavy breasts – breasts she had, with the help of her aunts and an array of herbs concocted together, managed to shrink to a not-too-revealing size. It was a masterpiece in deceit. Zhondezi tried to get her to face him but all she did was answer his advances in a soft-spoken tone, "Like this and I will not be able to get our *kenjas*, boxes and everything else ready for tomorrow." To which he replied by introducing the subject.

"About going back with me to Burwandai, you don't need to worry yourself." That got her attention, enough to make her turn and face him.

"What do you mean?"

"Sit down, honey you see, you have to live here - for now. Don't you worry, I will put up a decent structure for you near my in-law's house..."

"You mean my dad?"

"Do I have any other in-law here?" His smile was met with a caustic stare from Scolastica.

"I promise it's just for a while to give me enough time to put things in their proper place before the arrival of the queen of my heart to her palace."

At that point Scolastica's mind had begun to play havoc on her, all over again.

'It must be Ekodinge' was the first thought that had crossed her mind. 'He sure knows how much I love Ekodinge and so does not want me anywhere close to Burwandai.' But was that reason enough for any newly-wed to be cool about having his new bride next to him? Why would someone who had obsessed over her before their marriage suddenly be so eager to keep his wife at bay? In fact, anyone hearing this proposition was bound to wonder if this man was one of those who routinely sold their manhood to *Mami Wata*, the evil goddess of the underwater, in exchange for wealth and power. Although she possessed ample evidence to the contrary, including her aching waist and backside, still she feared the consequences of the devastating rumour mills. If that was how it was going to be, she told herself, she would endeavour to make the best of the situation. At this sudden coincidence of wishes, she smiled inside her. Come to think of it, there was this side of her that was not in the least keen on going back to Burwandai, after all. True, she would find it tough to stand to look Ekodinge in the face again. Not that she felt guilty about this – after all, he too had gone ahead and got married to another woman. It would just be an awkward situation, for both, no doubt. Her disdain over the position of co-wife was public knowledge, almost, and here she was being offered a golden opportunity to technically opt out of that role. It was one thing to share the man, it was quite another to live under the same roof with her co-wives, or more aptly, enemies-in-arms. She wondered how her father, mother and their contemporaries pulled it off with seemingly no sweat at all.

Sad, perplexed and happy all at once, she simply replied, "How come?" To which her husband just sat, staring all about him, his left arm wrapped around her right arm.

It would not be until several years after this incident that she would finally piece together what to her appeared to be the real motives for this man's bizarre decision the week of their wedding. Her two co-wives had, in a rare moment of unity, threatened Zhondezi to not only cut back on their conjugal duties toward him but to also extend the same courtesy to his manhood, and to finish Scolastica if she dared step her foot in their matrimonial home.

"There is something not straight with this *ashawo*," they had intimated without any further details. *Ashawo*, they dared call her! Indeed, some tongues were like a river, whose downward flow cannot be prevented, and many were the adults in this town who knew exactly whom that referred to. With the umbrella of marriage over their heads, it was easy for them to be flippant and to castigate the other for not having the good judgement to possess and carry an umbrella during a rainstorm. Marriage, how haughty and sanctimonious it can be – as if husbands were bought and sold in the town market. To their shock, their husband had

43

capitulated, or so it seemed, way beyond their wildest dream, thereby leaving them, and all who had heard about his reaction, even more perplexed. He had decided to have his new wife live in Tobeningo. 'After all, my business takes me all over the place, it will be nice to have a warm blanket everywhere one spends the night.' His brother, upon learning about the decision, had stomped his home and counselled against 'leaving a goat to be guarded by lions.' To no avail. Later, the women would switch to intimating it was all nothing but one huge, satanic plot hatched by the witch of a woman to snatch Zhondezi from them. They had even gone to Scolastica's aunt and pleaded with her to talk their man out of the idea. They even considered employing the services of a *mungang*, which, in this town, was like looking for the toilet when confronted with a heavy bout of diarrhoea. But none of this would ruffle Zhondezi's feathers.

All this much Scolastica had culled through the grapevine.

****

With her husband barely around, Scolastica got married to work and enterprise in Tobeningo. It was as if she was engaged in a practice run of sorts. She dabbled into anything that could fetch a penny. In no time she was rubbing shoulders with the big market women of this town – and ruffling some feathers in the act. Day in and day out she was fighting hard to make Ekodinge a distant patchwork in the fabric of her mind. After all, Ekodinge too had done same, hadn't he? If not, why had he not bothered to try to get in touch? She quickly adjusted her thought. From what she had gathered, he was now married, and so was she. Every now and then, she resolved to let sleeping dogs lie – which was more times than usual.

Chapter Six

It was late afternoon when the headmaster of his former school showed up at his father's house. That he came unannounced was not a surprise; no one around here ever did otherwise. Furthermore, it was market day, a day people were wont to take a few liberties at whatever, a day when, as Ekodinge's friend always jokingly maintained, even the lame walked. That the headmaster should be visiting his dad at all, well, that he found unusual. After all, what business did the tortoise have with the cock? His mind at once began to get the better of him. Committed any mischief or crime lately? None he could recall. In fact, ever since the day he had been thoroughly flogged by this same fellow – his class teacher then – for stealing a tin of sardines from Mr Ajabala's shop he had been a model pupil. Okay, he also got into trouble the day the owner of a nearby farm, fed up with his losses, marched to his school one afternoon and identified him as one of the gang that for the proverbial ninety-nine days had incessantly plundered his sugarcane farm. Well, all that was many years ago now; he was now a college graduate and this man no longer commanded any authority over him. Wrong again, for in these parts, one never graduated from the shadows of one's teacher, let alone headmaster. These folks exercised their role as gatekeepers to the heavily sought-after *mukala*'s world with a next-to omnipotent power of life, and definitely limb, over their pupil-subjects. Ganchu conceded that alone not only entitled his presence in any Burwandai compound at any time but also to be received like a chief, if he so wished. Still, the uncertainty surrounding the man's presence kept Ganchu's heart palpitating.

After the customary greetings, the headmaster wanted to know if he had had his results yet. Ganchu was part of the graduating first batch of Burwandai Government College and it is fair to say there was a lot of anticipation over the entire Native Authority area on just how these results would turn out.

"Not yet, Sir," he obliged

"I see, and will you pass?'

What was this fellow up to anyway with this line of questioning? Unlike the previous headmaster, if one believed the grapevines, J.N.T. Mbotankeh had established for himself the reputation of one who was not keenly interested in the welfare of his pupils, past or future, only the present.

"Well, Sir, I think I did the best I could. I hope it is good enough for a pass."

"You think, you hope, where is your confidence, young fellow? The philosophy of positive thinking, you do remember something about that, or do you not?"

Neither he nor his victim said anything for a while, then, "And what do you intend to do now that you have finished college?"

"I hope to...no, I will go to the regional capital, Motombolombo and drop off some letters of application in the government offices."

"Maybe I could secure a job – as a clerk or a pupil teacher."

"I see, clerk or a pupil teacher. You don't sound to me like a young man who knows exactly what he wants, let alone one that has passed through the august institution I now oversee. Eh, what ever happened to your power of positive thinking? Did you or did you not learn that at my institution?" The mini-lecture was followed by another enervating moment of silence. What was this fellow up to?

Had he ever heard that if you threw a dragnet with huge holes out at sea you could end up catching a big fish but definitely no shrimps?

"A pupil teacher,' he repeated as he picked up from where he left, 'why teaching?"

'Oh no, you are not getting me on this one,' Ganchu heard himself vowing. How, he wasn't sure, but if it smelled a rat, it was sure a rat. But first he had to overcome the nausea he experienced over the man's spew. 'My institution my foot! As if this was some university.'

"It is an honourable profession, Sir, and I will be honoured if I could be part of it" he heard himself saying. He did not believe the mumbo-jumbo but it sounded good, and who knew, it could actually play in his favour with this man who, by every indication, was quite influential. At least, that was the air he carried around him.

"Honourable," the headmaster repeated, again. 'You don't think so? Well, that's your business; I gave it my best shot,' Ganchu said to himself.

"I did not see your father at the market square so I decided to come look for him at home" the headmaster switched.

"He left home since morning right after he returned from tapping his palms, but he should be back soon because he..."

"Do you know that for certain?"

The fountain of etiquette, here he was breaking one of his cardinal principles by rudely interrupting, Ganchu found himself thinking. Oh well, after all, what were midgets like himself if not minions in the eyes and at the service of the likes of Mister J.N.T Mbotankeh. No hard feelings

"Well, he has to sleep if he has to go hunting tonight," he replied.

"Well, I have come all this way, how can I go back without even seeing him? You go fetch him. And make it snappy!"

Spoken like the true dictator he was reputed to be. Where, on earth, was he to find his dad at this hour? Burwandai might not be a city but that did not make things any easier. For starters, he was dealing here with one of the, if not the most secretive person ever to walk this earth, who never let anyone in on his movements, when and where he ate – not even whether or not he engaged in any of the town's favourite pastimes. And did this stupid intruder not hear him mention 'farm, 'and with it the possibility of having to trek for miles to find his dad?

"I will be on my way right away, Sir," he answered the headmaster and took off.

Ganchu was lucky; they were back moments later. Ganchu wore a broad smile as if to pat himself for a job well done.

"Ah, headmaster, what a surprise to see you." After he, as of custom, inquired about his guest's health and that of his family, Ganchu's father added, "I hope nothing is the matter."

"Our people say when you see a frog in the daytime know it is pursuing something or something is pursuing it." Both men laughed. "But nothing of the sort, here, I assure you."

"Then, by all means, please do have a seat" and turning to Ganchu, he screamed, "Fix a seat for the headmaster, my friend, instead of standing there and staring at places like a pillar."

Their chairs dusted, both men sat down.

"Ah, what a day, headmaster," continued Ganchu's father. "It seems as if people all lose their heads whenever Kwanzaa rolls around." Then, again to his son, "Quick, run

50

to Mami Kwacha and tell her to fill this calabash with the best *kwacha* she has." Ganchu was once again on his heels as his dad continued to reiterate to his guest the vicissitudes of life at Kwanzaa time.

"It would appear everyone wants to strike deals to last seven more moon cycles over. Even people who have nothing to buy or sell, you see them all looking busy over nothing - like that your foolish banana inspector, eh, what's his name again?"

"Massa Mukwata!" they both intoned, and laughed.

Ganchu was back in a jiffy. You could tell from the look on his face he was still questioning the headmaster's motive. His dad split a large kolanut into several halves, threw a piece into his mouth, dropped the other halves in a wooden bowl, which he placed in front of his visitor.

"Massa, there is kola," he announced. The libation poured, host and guest took the first few gulps of *kwacha* and, almost in a synchronized move, placed their long bamboo cups on the table. Ekodinge apologized for the less than befitting welcome — say some special brand of *mukala* drink for his august visitor; he wore a kind of infantile look on his face as he did so. It was as if to say any man worth his name had to have something of that kind in his cupboard for such august occasions. The headmaster seemed to wave off the apology. Immediately, he bent forward his head, which meant Edokinge had to do same. All Ganchu could catch were isolated words to be of any significance: principal, *mukala*... and head nods.

The headmaster stood up as if to leave just as Jenje Moto showed up.

"Massa, this is such great news you have brought to my family, it cannot end here. I will certainly find time and come and see you." Ekodinge raised his hands and eyes to the heavens, and did a dance.

"However, there is one favour I would like to ask of you, Sir, before you go." He rushed to his bedroom, came out with some bag and beckoned to his guest, friend and son to follow him. They proceeded to the family tombs in the backyard.

"We gather here at this momentous hour to do that which for generations before us has been the means of our sustenance, the dawn of our days. And may it continue for generations yet unborn," he intoned.

"Indeed," the audience responded in a single voice.

"If we stand tall it is because we stand on the shoulders of those who have gone before us."

"From time immemorial, our ancestors have done this to underlie the unity of spirit of the trinity – the departed, the living and the unborn."

"True," the audience answered.

Ganchu knelt - was made to kneel – at the foot of his grandfather's tomb. His father stood behind him, and to the left of the tomb stood his friend, Jenje Moto. The headmaster, as special guest, stood on the right side. With himself first, he introduced everyone present.

"Should you encounter a mountain - even as tall as the Fongetafula – may it shrink to let you pass before rising again."

"Indeed,"

Ekodinge moved to the head of his father's tomb. Starring straight at the head of the tomb and as if addressing the one inside, he poured palm wine from a calabash, and spoke with each drop. "Tomorrow he leaves to go to the fountain of them who are next to our spirits. May he not only get there safely but drink abundantly from that fountain."

"Amen."

"And bring some back to us."

"Indeed," they answered again.

After he pinched some earth from the spot he had poured palm wine, the party went back inside. Later that evening Ekodinge, in the presence of his son who watched with rapt attention, wrapped the earth portion judiciously before handing it to Ganchu.

"You will not part from this throughout your stay in the *mukala*'s land." "It is from your mother and I."

Ganchu looked at his dad in disbelief but could not utter a word.

Chapter Seven

Francisca was an eye-catcher, although around her thirties and with three children to her apron. Returning from the farm that afternoon, she had suddenly collapsed in front of her kitchen. There was no one around. At first Ekodinge did not give much thought to this, thinking it was a mere case of fatigue. But when she would not wake after a while Ekodinge quickly jumped over the low hedge separating both compounds and rushed toward her. Going on his knees, he whacked himself on the forehead. Then, he squeezed her nostrils gently, brought his mouth down to hers and began pumping huge bouts of air into her, only stopping now and then to check her pulse. Pump, check, pump, check and then - nothing. He wiped a trickle of sweat off his face, turned his head around and his eyes met with those of a little boy who could be no more than five. The boy at once disappeared into the main house. The only thing Ekodinge could remember was that, from here, everything happened at break-neck speed. Ekodinge recalled having seen this child twice or thrice before. From what he had gathered, he was Francisca's son from a previous marriage and had arrived to live with his mother only recently. He was the source of bitter marital fights between Francisca and her husband. Ekodinge ascertained all of this only thanks to Burwandai's efficient gossip mill. He had fallen out with Francisca's husband after he had been accused of having an affair with the newly married Francisca. It was a rumour neither he nor the woman fought hard to refute. It was only upon the passing of his wife, several years down the road, that the two compounds had resumed exchanging greetings, albeit tepid. Here he was, beside the dead body of this woman with whom he now had an indisputable bond; whether or not it was real did not matter. He would be arrested, charged with murder, maybe convicted and condemned to die. He who had been honourably discharged from the King's army, who had saved a number of comrades in arms on the battlefields of Morocco and Mongolia; a modestly successful jack-of-all-trades, whose name had been circulating, if only in hushed tones, as the next member of *Etemzoh,* the prestigious group of titled men of his community, here he was, about to be reduced to nothingness. He did not need to be told. Over the years he had been witness to the weird manner with which the *mukala* administered justice – full of revenge and poor judgement. Instead of letting quarrelling folks duke it out in a wrestling match the *mukala* now had them locked up, making widows of their wives and orphans of their children. Instead of seeking healing for the community, he pitted one against another when he declared one man victor and the other loser

His mind was in tatters, oscillating between building up a defence and questioning the gods for forsaking him. Never before had he failed at any attempt at resuscitation; why now? Why would he kill the woman many believed he loved? And who among this town full of rumour mongers would even give him the benefit of doubt, let alone be prepared to take the stand in his defence? He would not willingly give in, he vowed.

Chapter Eight

She showed up at the premises of the Chairman way ahead of the members of the council. As she would later explain to her friend, it was all the culmination of pent-up frustration at the private manner this fellow was running the public affairs of Burwandai. She had tried, repeatedly, outside of the confines of meetings, to get him and other members of the council to give her an audience before them at one of their meetings. Each one she had approached was like throwing water on a duck. So, she had shelved the matter.

The meeting had hardly kicked off than she raised her hand. As they fumbled over whether protocol was being respected, Scolastica shot out, "Gentlemen, I would like to put down my name as one of the people to speak during today's meeting - yes, I want to talk about the situation of our market women."

The secretary eyed every man seated with him at the high table – rickety, unpolished, but high all the same; it was clear he was begging for some help out of a visibly awkward situation. Then, he spoke into the ear of the Chairman of the Native Authority, after which he looked up at Scolastica and mumbled something to the effect that protocol was not being respected. The Chairman, for his part, took one look at her and Native Authority answered, "Request denied." When she repeatedly sought to get him to explain the reason for turning down her request, the Chairman simply got up from his chair and left the room. He was hardly outside than two young men burst into the room and bundled Scolastica, screaming and kicking, out.

A moon-cycle later Scolastica got up one morning to find one of the chairman's acolytes at her doorstep. She did not even give him time to begin.

"What is it this, don't you fellows ever sleep? Always going around looking for fresh prey, eh?"

"Master says intelligence reports have reached him to indicate that you are about to cause trouble in this town, that you should, with immediate effect, forget this your stupid idea before he does something you will regret," the messenger spoke at last.

Scolastica, her hands at akimbo, fixed a gaze on him, neither uttering a word nor moving. It was as if she was suspecting this fellow knew something. For a moment, after he left, she wondered if she should go ahead with the plan.

Then, on one market day, without any warning - and in obvious disregard of the warning she had received from the chairman – there was Scolastica, going all over the market. She approached a woman, uttered something into her ear, followed by a nod and a wink, and then proceeded to the next. Yes, it was on that magic day – market day. The next thing the folks of Burwandai saw was a sea of market women marching up to the Chairman's compound. Some carried branches, others leaves. Most were simply shouting, 'the tax is too high, reduce it! Build more stalls before you chase us from selling in the open!'

'We will complain to Motombolombo,' the protesters threatened.

Chapter Nine

Ganchu was leaning by the window of his apartment. This was not just a feat, not even a dream, but a true miracle. Here he was in Lancashire – or close to it – a twenty-something African colonial subject, who had spent all his life reciting 'God save the king' on Empire days and every other public occasion he could recall. In a way he now felt like he, and not the empire, was ruling the waves. Yes, God save this humble subject, for there would be no king but for the subjects. His academic program had progressed smoothly and soon he would be the first one from the region with a Bachelor's degree. No, it was not one for unmarried young men. Still and in true testament to his weirdness, the *mukala* called it Bachelor's degree!

He could not but recall the many word games he played as a kid. You threw out a word and had your opponents figure out what each letter stood for. The combined outcome, most of the time, did not make sense; but who said sense was of any essence when one was having fun. And yes, Lancashire was a favourite test word: *Let All Nations Come And See How I Rule England.* It did not matter the fact that literally every baby across town knew what it meant, it remained a regular in these mental quizzes. Such was their stamp on life, the age of innocence.

Ganchu lived on the third floor of a student hostel. The building looked like something out of the Victorian era. He shared the floor with three other students from the vast empire. Lion Coast he had heard before, but it was the first time he was learning about some two island countries, Triyanti and Barbadinia. All four bedrooms faced out unto a common living area which had a toilet and bathroom to one end. The common area was also equipped with a refrigerator and a stove, both kerosene-powered. There was a long sofa; Ganchu did not need to ask as he was near certain the mahogany that constituted the edges of this chair had to be from one of the tropical colonies of the empire – maybe his own.

It was Saturday morning. All floor mates had just finished writing their exams. There was not much to do except one were of Ganchu's disposition, in which case it was time to pursue some extra reading – all of which had to have a bearing on his school program! It might a holiday break but there could never be anything as studying too hard – not when one felt like the hope of an entire Native Authority region lay on one's shoulders. But not even this could take away the loneliness of the Christmas season and the pain and havoc of snow – not even prayers -for the quick resumption of classes. Their senior colleague from Triyanti, who had family somewhere in the country, had left the day before to go spend time with them. Good riddance; the holier-than-thou type did nothing but make Ganchu and the others feel their place in hell had been booked solid.

For breakfast, Ganchu helped himself to a slice of stale bread and a cup of tea – maybe tea from his place again, he thought. Then he picked up an old newspaper and went back to bed. He would give himself this weekend, at least, to relax before hitting the books again. He began to re-read the *News from the Colonies'* section, dozing in between paragraphs. It was almost noon when he was awakened by a knock on the door. He jumped out of bed and flung open the door.

"Good day Mister Ganchu," she greeted softly.

"Good...good day, and what a surprise, Mrs..." answered a perplexed Ganchu.

"Emerald is fine," she helped him out of his moment of hesitation. And I am sorry for showing up without an appointment or something of the sort. You'd agree with me, it's not very..."

"English?"

"You can say that too," she agreed.

"Honestly, I thought it was one of my floor mates." There was an awkward moment of silence during which both simply stood there looking at each other.

"If this is a bad time I could come..."

"Oh, I'm sorry, please do come in." he moved to one side to allow her heavy frame to slide through, just as he cast a quick look backwards to take stock of his unkempt apartment. Not that he himself looked any better. For a moment he could not tell which worried him more; the apartment or the extra corporal baggage she seemed to be carrying since the last time he saw her. Or could it be her visibly thick winter apparel? While his mind fumbled, he struggled to pick up his dirty clothing strewn all over the place.

"Here, let me help you with that," she said, as she struggled to take off her coat and place...somewhere. His assessment of extra baggage, earlier on, was confirmed!

"It's okay," he answered, slightly tense, maybe at being caught on his weak side.

"Where are my manners, dear me?" he continued, forcing a smile, as he quickly dumped his load to one end of the room thinking 'Better there than all over the floor,' and as he struggled to catch her coat on its way down.

"Let me please have your coat." Both of them instinctively reached down at the same time in a futile bid to catch it. Cold hands!

'Heavy frame, alright,' as he took yet another look at her.

"You are welcome to my humble abode, and please have a seat, Mrs" he announced with the airs of a protocol officer in training.

"Emerald," she corrected once again, then added, "Well, thank you. For a moment there I felt like I had caught you at a bad time," she answered. And for the first time since she arrived, she showed a broad smile behind a clean pair of teeth.

'Easy for you to say,' thought Ganchu, as she squeezed into one of the two chairs by the table. Ganchu sat on the edge of his bed, which gave a squeak. 'Now, what next?' He was not the conversational type – especially not when he was caught off his element.

"Wow, am I surprised to see you," he said.

"Why, you shouldn't be."

"What is it, about two years?"

"Something of the sort."

"Boy, am I completely dry or what!"

"I beg your pardon?" she asked.

"I'm sorry, I mean I don't have anything worth serving you. I was only planning to go pick a few groceries later this afternoon."

He was up on his feet, a small carton of Tetley tea in his hand.

"Oh, don't worry about it, tea will be just fine. Nothing like a hot cup of English tea to keep you in good spirits on a day like this, eh."

'English tea, indeed; as if one can grow tea anywhere in this damn cold place' thought Ganchu. He excused himself and stepped in the common area to boil water for tea. She was standing at the window and staring outside when he returned with the kettle of water. Tea served, she took two sips and commented, "Wow, this is richly brewed."

Another English exaggeration – maybe it was only in the heart of English country that boiling water required some special skill. Ganchu had concluded long ago these people had a flare for exaggeration; they spoke about the weather, to the exclusion, almost, of everything else. They basked to exhaustion in the shadow of something they called freedom. It was, to them, like some pill or intoxicating drink which they – and they alone – had discovered. They exaggerated some more even by the way they refused to open their mouths when they spoke. As if that were not enough, they exaggerated over the true ownership of their so-called Tetley tea. It was as if they lived oblivious to the wise one's counsel, of virtue turning into vice if one stretched it too much. Still, he felt good as she was obviously working hard to put him at ease.

"You won't ask me how I found you?"

"I was going to," he lied, although the issue had crossed his mind at least once since she got in. She reminded him how he had told her his address several months back.

"Besides, you can't be that hard to locate; after all, how many blacks live in this area? I wonder, how did you manage to get an apartment in an area like this?"

"Because not many blacks live in the area, you mean?"

"That too."

"Actually, one of our professors at the university arranged this for us."

"And they don't give you trouble?"

"Who?"

"You know...the..."

"Oh, I see," Ganchu helped her out, "they would have to find you to give you trouble, right?" She stared at him, incredulous.

"I mean, I spend most of my days, and nights, I might add, on campus."

"You don't say." It was followed by another round of silence, then "If it is not an imposition, I could accompany you to do your grocery shopping whenever you are ready." She spoke without looking at him.

Ever since she arrived Ganchu was dying to find out about her husband; it was a curiosity founded on a deep concern over his own safety. First, he would like to know why he had not seen them in church over such a long time.

"Fred got transferred to another city."

"So you are back in town?"

"You can say I am..." Her tone was lackadaisical, even laconic. He thought he heard her say 'I' but could not muster the courage - yet - to ask her. Sensing the look of uncertainty on his face, she helped him out, "We lost him."

"What, when, where...I mean, how?"

"In a training exercise...a helicopter crash...in the Midlands."

"I am truly sorry to hear that," Ganchu said.

"Thank you, my dear," she answered, paused, then continued, "we miss him dearly."

'We, who?' Another mental challenge for Ganchu, who could only repeat himself, "I am indeed sorry at your loss."

"It's okay." She ran her arm down his and he collected the empty tea saucers from the table. A most comforting gesture of empathy, only that he was supposed to be the one extending it, he thought. Back in the room, Ganchu again sat on the edge of his bed. He was experiencing a strange sense of calmness.

"So, when did this happen?"

She answered all his journalistic enquiries on the matter, and more, then, "Enough of this moodiness," she announced as she quickly switched topics. "Tell me about school."

"Well, what can I say?"

"At least, assure me it's alright."

"I'm doing my best, that much I'm certain about. In fact, if things stay on track, I will be a graduate in just over a year from now." And, for the afterthought, "can hardly wait to bid farewell to this white powder stuff." They both looked out the window again. Her faint smile could hardly conceal the fact that he had struck a nerve, perhaps a raw one? She got up, slowly paced to the window, pulled the curtain completely to one end. The brightness belied the cold.

"Would you come....Boy, I don't have..." They both spoke at the same time.

"I'm sorry, you were about to say something," she turned her head only briefly to look at Ganchu, still perched to the edge of his bed; then, it was back again outside.

"Oh, I was merely about to apologize for not having any groceries at home."

"Again I say not to worry...we can pick up a few items first thing tomorrow morning."

She turned her head around again. There was a confused, almost stern look from Ganchu.

"Or maybe later tonight," she tried to minimize the shock.

The mention of 'tonight' hit Ganchu – the toilet! Unless she was like these missionaries he was used to back home, she sure would ask to use the toilet sometime between now and tonight, thought Ganchu. He immediately got up, fetched the tin of disinfectant – one hundred per cent pure *Izal* – excused himself and left the room. No, there was never any problem between him and his hostel mates over the cleaning and cleanliness of the toilet. Nor was it his turn to clean it but he just needed added assurance the place was fit for a lady.

While he was gone, Emerald left the window, went over and stretched herself on the opposite side of small bed. She locked both palms together, placed them on the pillow and gently let her head rest in the lock.

"Where about is your tap? I need to go fetch a glass of water," she said as soon as he stepped back into the room.

'Are you trying me or something?' He vocalized it not quite the same way he thought. "I could call that an affront to my gentlemanly upbringing, you know." He smiled, and added, "Of course, I will get you some water."

He was off with an aluminium cup in hand, as he heard her say, "I just don't want to be a burden to you, that's all."

With Ganchu back, she sat up, accepted the cup of water, took a sip and placed the cup on the floor.

"So, what are you up to these days?" he asked, handing her the water.

From the way she raised her head, the question took her by surprise.

Ganchu moved over to a table chair. She did not answer right away. Instead, she closed her eyes for a moment, then opened them, looked at Ganchu and smiled. It did not look like a joyous smile but it a smile all the same.

"Just trying to keep body and spirit together," she answered despondently. Then, a lengthy silence engulfed the apartment.

"If I invite you to a function in our church next week will you come?"

"You are talking to me?" It was his turn to be off.

"I don't see anyone else in this room."

"And what was that you said again?"

"I must say you are pretty off-minded; anything that I can help with?" She sounded genuine, as she got up, walked to the table and placed an arm on Ganchu's shoulder.

Out of the blue, and unable to explain why, he suddenly found himself thinking about his mother. Ever since he embarked on this adventure this had become one of his many worries, a distraction, if not an obsession. Who was she? Where was she and how was she doing? Why had she abandoned him? He had not been completely in the dark on answers to these questions – if only in sketches – thanks to Burwandai's effective rumour mill. No, he had nothing but kind memories about the mother who raised him, however short a time that lasted. He was bound to call her 'mother', for as a child, did he not belong to all the women of the community? What he blamed was his seen-and-not-heard status, which did not permit him to ask any questions – and get answers – whilst growing up in Burwandai.

He shook his head to snap out of his thought, and blamed the woman now in his room for partially fuelling this flame with the near-motherly manner she was now behaving toward him.

****

They had been going steady for over half a year now.

"It's been nearly six months since I sent the telegram and still no reply," Ganchu fumed as he got up and paced to the refrigerator, opened it and took out a bottle of beer. He uncorked it and finished its contents in a few huge gulps.

"This can't be my father; even if he were down to his last shilling he would make sure he sent someone to Motombolombo, or went himself, to reply to such an important letter." He had been at this for the better part of an hour and even Emerald's patience was wearing thin.

"What is Moto-bo?

"What?"

"I mean what you just said."

"Oh, Motombolombo. It's not the first time you are hearing this, is it? Whatever, that's where the post office for the entire Native Authority area is found." "Mo-to-bo-lom-bo," he picked the syllables one by one as he forced a smile, apparently at the fact that he knew she could not pull this one through.

"You must take it easy, dear," she tried to advice. "I am certain there is a logical explanation somewhere, somehow." She followed that up with "And have you thought about what you intend to do?"

"Go home!"

"What?"

"Go home, that's what I'm going to do."

"You are not going to leave us here all by ourselves, are you?"

"What?"

"You heard me, you are not going alone."

****

In her mid-to-late thirties, Emerald was the mother of a young daughter. She had first met Ganchu in her church shortly after he arrived to study at Lancashire and had almost instantly taken an interest in his welfare. As a member of the parish's social and welfare committee, she would always insist that he stay on for the after-service refreshments every Sunday. It was a solicitude that did not find favour with her husband, mother and other members of her family -

especially after she invited him to their home at Easter (his first in the country) for some good old home cooking, as she put it. It had been a heated exchange with her mother, who had not minced words.

'You can chat, smile and even share a cup of our good old English Tetley with them at the church if you like, but to bring them to your home, ugh, it's like inviting him to your innermost sacred chamber.'

'And what is wrong about that, mother?'

'You dare ask me what is wrong about that! I see you have been swallowed by some African juju spell. You are lucky you have a fine husband, but I just pray he does not change his mind about you one of these days.'

She had, as a result, withdrawn the proposed invitation and cut back on her socializing with Ganchu, to the extent that she did not bother to tell him when they moved from Lancashire.

Now, her mother and husband gone, in their respective ways, the coast was clear for her to anchor her canoe – and whatever else.

70

Chapter Ten

Ekodinge was lost in his thoughts and did not even acknowledge the greeting of the girls. He had a lot going on in his life at the same time and not enough room, it seemed, to manoeuvre. Here he was, like a baby monkey learning the ropes all over again. As Burwandai's most famous hunter his life and thoughts seemed to revolve around animals. More so at this hour. Yes, the hunter was now the hunted. As though that was not enough, he was beginning this new life during what were supposed to be the near sunset years of his life, in a strange land among strange people and with a completely new identity to boot. Most troublesome was this thing about a new name. In his third month here and he still was unused to it. And who could blame him? A name was a man's identity, part of his being. He felt like a kid going to school for the first time, which in itself conjured up the image of an underdog - always at the tail-end and mercy of teacher with all the authority in the world at the end of a cane. He might not know who the authority was but he sure knew who it was not. From his movements being curtailed to the disguise he had to wear on a daily basis, he was the condemned prisoner all alone with his executioner who is only too eager getting ready to tighten the noose around his neck and pull the log from under his feet.

Then he heard the all-too familiar conversation outside. Scolastica was arguing with a customer.

"How many times will I tell you I no longer sell *mimbo* at home?" "If you want *mimbo* you should come to the market square."

Stubbornly, the lanky fellow simply pulled a bamboo chair and landed on it before his dangling legs could betray him.

"Since when, and who issued that authority?' 'Is it that foolish what-is-his-name chairman? Because if he is the one, tell him he is sacked – as from today."

"So, you are the only man in this town who does not know?"

"Me, not know that your so-called chairman? Look, tell him this is the real chairman, you hear?" He thumped his chest for emphasis, and for a moment it looked as if his fingers were glued to his chest.

"I am telling you I no longer sell at home..."

"A big, fat lie – as fat as a fly!" Words only a perfect drunkard could articulate. "Oh yes, if it is not a lie, why has Matango not gone around town with his gong to inform us the people who matter?" And for an icing on the cake, "it's government for *di* people, with *di* people, by *di* people, according to..."

"Oh, shut up your beak," cut in Scolastica as the fellow gave out a heavy combo. The belch and the fart were so heavy that Scolastica actually turned around to look at this pig that just then had intruded into the yard. Back and forth they went until the tenacity of the drunkard worn her down.

"Okay, just this one, and please do hurry and leave," she said handing him a two-litre tumbler of kwacha. "And do keep it down as I don't want anyone coming around here to bug me."

"Is there something in that house that you are itching to go to?" retorted the fellow as even Ekodinge chuckled, before frowning, from his prison hideout.

It was the eve of an important day on the Tobeningo calendar. As elsewhere, a lot happened on this day. Important deals were struck. A few serious fights were registered. Even relationships were made and unmade. And yes, Molekaya's tax collectors were sure to show up. Scolastica and daughters had been on their feet all day getting stuffs ready for market.

The sun had all but gone home to sleep. The sheep, goats, pigs and fowls were all coming home, as usual, after a long day of scavenging in the vicinity and beyond. But this woman's day was far from done. She was a woman used to being on her toes ever since her husband Zhondezi had died leaving her with two young girls to raise. The forty-something had developed into a business-savvy woman. It was strange to see her, at any time, not doing something.

The drunkard was about to leave when Scolastica emerged back from indoors.

"And where do you think you are going, mister eh...? Have you paid me?"

"Customer, ah ah, it's just between you and I. Don't you know me any longer?"

"No, I do not know you!"

"I will pay you tomorrow."

"I will pay you tomorrow," she mimicked through her nasal passage rather than her mouth. "You haven't even paid your previous bill, have you? And you dare to talk of 'I will pay you tomorrow."

In the end, it proved to be another futile effort on her part. For some reason she could not figure, this particular fellow always seemed to have his way with her. Maybe it had to do with the fact that she could always get him, when sober, to do whatever chores she needed to have done – chores that more than compensated for his debt. The fellow was soon on his way humming, cursing, croaking and talking to himself and just about anyone – and animal – he ran into.

"Who was that?" Ekodinge asked when Scolastica came in.

"Who else but the self-styled president of the national team of drunkards – sorry, drinkers – of Tobeningo." They both laughed.

The look on Ekodinge's face could devour Scolastica, who pretended not to notice. She meticulously dropped some last minute ingredients into the huge containers of kwacha and then went about her other tasks. Happily, thought Ekodinge, she was still holding her own after all the years of family tragedies and hard labour as the vagaries of time had taken only a slight toll on her body. Two shallow furrows on her face, wrinkles on the back of her palms, tummy and a rear end that had protruded backwards only slightly were nothing compared to a great many of the town's women. What she lacked in physical beauty – not that it amounted to much – she amply made for with her grace. Ekodinge was particularly thankful that most crucial aspect of her anatomy protruded as sturdy as before from her chest. Then, his mind drifted to Jenje Moto, his friend back in Burwandai, who often joked he needed to feel something substantial between his fingers every time these came in contact with the upper symbol of womanhood.

Man and woman were now reunited yet Ekodinge could not help but feel remorse over the many years of unfulfilled love.

As he admired her with his eyes and mind, the latter took him back to that fateful day in Burwandai many moon cycles back, and to Francisca, the architect, in spite of her, of his current tribulations.

****

He was interrupted in his thoughts by a tap on the shoulder, "My dear, your food is ready."

Without notice, nor thought, he pulled Scolastica toward him, onto his lap and found himself fondling her ear lobes.

"Oh, please stop,' she feigned a protest and as if to pull away, 'people might be watching."

"And so? Let them all come and I will give each a pair of iron eyes."

"For someone who is or should be, you know what, that's not far from cavalier, if you ask me."

"Good, I did not ask you."

He knew she was right and that he could not take too many chances. Still, he hated to be reminded of the precarious nature of this his present existence. He found this particular remark an exaggeration of the tallest order, and he let her know about it. 'Right inside my own, I mean the house,' was all he said. After a deafening silence during which man and woman just sat starring at and away from each other, Scolastica was ready to thicken her defence.

"Your food is getting cold," she began.

"But she looks and feels hot to me."

"What did you just say?" as she turned her head swiftly to face him.

"Ah, woman, don't pretend you did not hear."

"Hear what, you rascal, don't you have passed the time for that?'

Ekodinge countered, "For what, my friend?"

Scolastica sought to divert, "Tomorrow is a big market day".

"And so?"

"What if I fall asleep in the market?"

"Hah, my people, I implore you to come and hear this one! That's like saying..."

"...Seriously, don't you ever get tired after all these years?"

"Months, you mean? You are not counting all these years, I mean decades, that I did not set my eyes on you, not even sure if you were still alive, are you?"

For a while, it seemed the prey had succeeded to lure herself away from the hunter.

"But all kidding aside, what are going to do?"

"Why don't we cross that bridge when we get there," he answered as his hands struggled to resume their most important task.

"No, now. That is what I have never...about you"

"Liked?" he offered.

"...never serious even when you know you have to. always leaving things to chance....this your no-worry-no-hurry posture, well, might have some merit...sometimes...but, I needn't tell you that is how come the Germans lost this land." Her forehead was strained as she picked her words.

"Never serious, never worried? Are you talking about me or someone else?"

Then he reminded her of, as he put it, the trials and tribulations that he went through all these years as he struggled to locate her.

To which she countered, "Are you sure it was me or your son you were worried about? After all, you were comfortably caught in the dazzle and trance, tied to the *kabba* – and I dare not mention what else – of your new wife to bother about me."

He pulled his thigh from under Scolastica, almost sending her to the floor and as he shoved her away from him. "If that is supposed to be your idea of I-don't-know-what, I take deep exception to it."

"I am sorry." Ekodinge just walked.

"Haven't I said I am sorry?" Still, silence.

"And may the spirits continue to keep a soft spot for her."

The balm soothed Ekodinge; he turned his head briefly to eye Scolastica. The cat-woman seized the moment and planted a kiss on Ekodinge's left cheek, followed by a hug that would not end. Ekodinge resumed his assignment, sitting her on a bench and while beside her, sliding a hand under Scolastica's *kabba*.

"Is this Kaminata's or her sister's *kabba*?" he said.

She threw a strange look at him for this strange question and then followed it up with a "Why?"

"Not enough elbow room underneath." Smiles.

Gently, she pulled his hand back out.

"I am sorry, dear, not possible." They looked each other in the eye, she nodded and he understood. Then, she disappeared into the kitchen; there was another pot of kwacha cooking to attend to. Kaminata stepped in after her. Mother at once picked up on the sullenness of her daughter.

"You look like the weight of this house is on your shoulders. What is the matter, my dear?

"Everyone is making fun at Katema at school," Kaminata ventured.

"Why?" Scolastica asked, in a concerned voice.

"Eh, I don't have all the details, really."

"You don't know but you know that someone – or everyone – is making fun at your sister. Now, look here, my friend, I have more important things to do than worry over the pranks you kids play at school."

"Even when they are saying a man is living with her mother who is not her husband?"

"Will you shut up your dirty mouth, you trouble-maker, before I make you lose it forever?" she screamed, as her eyes – and then her daughter's -instinctively focused in the

77

direction of the main house. The thunder in her voice was matched only by the deep sense of fright in her heart; someone might have overheard, as she hurriedly looked about her, rushing out of the kitchen and into the yard, to make sure that was not the case. Despite all the precaution she thought she had taken, her secret of secrets was now in the open – the family oil spilled for any passer-by to lick. She was lamenting why her life seemed to revolve around putting out one fire after another. Still, she had to, she told herself, adopt the attitude of a fisherman caught in the middle of a tidal wave, with no option but to seek to paddle his canoe away from the storm – forward, sideways, or even backwards. And if this was any indication, she had to beware of even the shore for it could foreshadow danger. This one was a hot potato she had to handle with extreme care.

Chapter Eleven

It was obvious Ekodinge was enjoying this time off night-time hunting trips. He had not said why, only that he just needed to make up for the lost time. Comfortably ensconced in his laps was Scolastica. Her mind was looping from one fondly reverie to another; how, back in Burwandai, she always seemed to get a kick out of doing or saying something that angered Ekodinge – so much so that she actively began to incorporate that into her routine. Getting him annoyed made him girlish, and she liked that. But she remained always careful not to cross the line. Then, it was on to the many things that had attracted her to him from the first day she moved to Burwandai to live with her aunt, bless her soul. Older than her by no more than five years, she determined, he was youthful, exceptionally quiet – unlike his best buddy, Jenje Moto, whom she had, without a moment's hesitation, nicknamed Burwandai Talking Drum. It was a nickname even Ekodinge could not resist, eventually transforming it to *BTD – Beat 'till dawn*. Ekodinge was not particularly good at nor did he seem interested in most of the things that occupied the minds, nights and time of boys his age, such as fishing and hunting expeditions for birds, squirrels and rat mole – activities that often meant skipping school – generalized truancy, games and, of course, girls. He was smart, or so Scolastica had heard, much in demand by the chief, his councillors and just about anyone who relied on his services as a letter-writer – services for which he would receive nothing more than, often, a hand of bananas as compensation. It did not take long before the Sissy-just-come began exhibiting this unusual routine: she would show up after school in his neighbourhood, five streets away, her school bag slung across her neck and in between her budding breasts, would stroll up and down the street hoping to catch a glimpse of Ekodinge and present her problem – schoolwork - for his help. When that did not work, she would always manage to get her auntie to send her to Ekodinge's mother on one errand or another. It took a while but finally, the patient hunter had warmed her way into the heart of Ekodinge's mother who began to address her 'my daughter,' to the visibly pretentious disapproval of her son. Often, she would run into Jenje Moto, out to check on his friend, who wasted no time to bare his soul to her – to which the otherwise polite girl would respond with a soft smile, and a steady gaze on the nuisance, head to toe. Ekodinge found her attractive, even as most of his peers lied they did not. That she was of kindred spirit only added feathers to her crown in his eyes. She had eyes that slightly resembled a cat's but which did not, in a significant way, diminish her beauty. The eyes were a constant reason for scornful teases from the other girls. Oh, how that nature that protects can also, in one moment, turn around and kill with devastation!

Before she knew it, she had dozed off.

The tap on her shoulder was light, as the voice, as soft as a starling's, continued, "This is where you are going to spend the night?"

"Oh my, have I been dreaming or what!" She gently lifted herself from the sofa from which she had been comfortably laid by Ekodinge.

"Where are the girls?"

"Gone to sleep."

"Don't tell me it's that late. And that young naughty lady did not bother you for a story."

"Does the monkey ever spare a ripe banana?" joked Ekodinge. "Of course, I told her one, and I bet you, today's was a special one."

"Special, eh?"

"About a famous wrestler," he puffed.

Scolastica looked into his eyes, in disbelief.

"By Jove, I can't believe this, that was exactly...anyway, never mind."

"I would have told you but it appears as if you have heard the story before." He led her to the bedroom.

Once in, she dipped her hand inside her dress in between her breasts and pulled out a small bundle which she untied.

"Here, the money for the antelope," Scolastica said as she handed Ekodinge a note and some coins. He looked at her and screamed, "After several sleepless nights in the forest this is all I get?"

He sought to reassure himself, "For both antelopes, you said?"

"There is a lot of game out there this time of year; we're even lucky, I'd say."

"How do you know? Are you a hunter?"

"Ah, I am the one who goes to the market daily; I see it."

"Well, I hope you don't go out there and accept the first offer that is made to you only to come here to tell me about abundance of game."

He began to wonder if things would not have been different had he been the one out there selling his game. Still, deep down, he had to admit that Scolastica was doing quite an amazing job. It was not that many months since she had suddenly been thrust into this all too new role of game dealer. She felt angry Ekodinge did not seem to appreciate this. True, her kwacha business had boomed ever since she began to have a steady supply of bush meat, fresh and smoked, that her customers so craved for as an appetizer to drinking. But it was a role she was carrying out at great risk, even to her person. Of all the things she had undertaken to facilitate Ekodinge's entry into this line of business in Tobeningo, none had been as daring and risky as acquiring the gun for him. The *mukala* edict against gun ownership by natives was still in place, and the new government, in a fervour of nationalism, had relaxed it to allow for the ownership and limited use of locally made guns – at funeral celebrations only. It was a restriction that was flouted almost as soon as it came into force. But never in public, which made securing one for Ekodinge seem like a camel going through the eye of a needle. Every intermediary she had contacted had raised an eyebrow of suspicion, interrogated her repeatedly why she, a woman, needed a gun. None would bulge until she revealed everything, they each vowed. One or two folks in the Native Authority office even intimated if, for a woman who was gun-shopping, she had not had a hand in the death of her husband. It was all music to the ear of the chairman of the Native Authority who had tried to use this palm oil to ease the flow of some roasted plantain down his throat – backing down, only temporarily, after Scolastica called his bluff.

"Need I remind you," Scolastica answered Ekodinge gravely, "of what it took for me to secure for you the delicate tools for this business - to the extent that I am still an object of suspicion in this town to this day."

"What suspicion?" Ekodinge demanded, his interest roused as much by the thought of his cover being blown as by this woman getting into any kind of trouble. "Is there any trouble?"

"Has it occurred to you that there might be a few questions as to where I get such a steady supply of bush meat from?"

"It's none of anybody's business."

"Again, easy for you to say," she retorted, and added, "why do you think all these people insist on coming to drink here even after having been told business has move to the market square?"

"Are you trying to say I am the reason you are asking customers not to come here any longer?"

"What do you mean by that?"

"Did you yourself not say it was because the chairman and the Native Authority had warned you to stop conducting business at home?"

"Again, you are evading the point."

"And you are being paranoid; otherwise, what are you insinuating?"

"Me, paranoid! Well, your guess is as good as mine."

They were going in circles; this much they both realized. She could not fathom why Ekodinge would not apologize; he usually did in these situations. Maybe he did not want to get it over with; she too dug in.

"Stop playing these your mental games now, woman."

"Okay, I think you should take over the whole sales aspect," she pronounced.

He jerked, turned his head and looked her straight in the eye, speechless. Then he burst out, "Are you crazy? What has come over you? I mean, do you comprehend the implications of what you are saying?"

"Completely."

She kept her cool, if only for this split moment.

"Since I don't make enough money you need to take charge - like every other man worth his salt around here, I'd say." With that, she stormed out of the bedroom.

So angry was she that she refused to return to the bedroom; well, she did return, but only to pick up a blanket and storm right out again.

Neither had much sleep that night, let alone make any attempt to appease the other. For the first time, Scolastica wondered if she had made the right decision to accept him back into her life. 'I should have called the bluff on this completion thing from day one,' she thought. 'What is it that I have not done on my own?'

The following day, they picked up from where they had left off the day before. It was not long past sundown. Ekondinge had just awoke from sleep and was getting his hunting gear ready. It was then that Scolastica stepped in and threw the first salvo, "I have to go to Burwandai as soon as possible,"

"You will do no such crazy thing," intervened Ekodinge.

"And why do you think it is a crazy thing? Obviously, no one around here seems willing or has the guts to go anywhere, so, I am volunteering."

She said it in the most lackadaisical of manners yet with all the emphasis she could muster. If he did not know better Ekodinge might have attributed it to a cyclical swing of mood. Maybe she was still not through with it and with him. Otherwise, why this departure from the script the finer details of which she had been the key architect. In fact, Ekodinge could figure nothing but praise for the extra mile she had gone in order to protect his old identity ever since the day he landed in town heavily disguised. He recalled how he had waited patiently behind some tall grasses by the road until spotting someone who looked like Scolastica. There was a girl with her and they chatted as they went along. He was not completely sure it was her, not having caught a good look at her face. However, he had decided it was then or never. He had double-checked on his disguise, slipped out of the bush, walked stealthily behind them for a stretch before calling out her name. He had gone on to spill the beans – after awkwardly detaching the duo from each other- as to his true identity to a visibly shocked woman.

"And why are so particular about going back to Burwandai?"

"Well," she began, "the situation has changed, hasn't it? Any time from now our son will be returning from the *mukala*'s land to mourn the passing of his father – as custom demands. And I am supposed to just sit here and wait for thunder to come and strike me dead, eh?"

"The spirits forbid! And who told you that?"

"Who told me what is not as important as seeking a way to stop him before a sacrilege is committed."

"Again, Scola, I ask you: who told you that?" He was getting edgy.

"I heard it through the grapevines." When Ekodinge focused his gaze of disbelief on her, she recanted, "Well, my auntie in Burwandai."

"Ha, ha, ha, where did I keep my drink?"

"You can laugh all you want."

He jumped to his feet and made for the door. Somehow, the thought of having his cover blown was less of a worry than being party to some hanky-panky. Just before he stormed out, she shouted, "And where do you think you are going, Ekodi? Why can't we settle this as mature adults."

He turned around and addressed her, "Let me get this straight, are we talking about the same aunt I know?" And not giving her room to respond, he fired another salvo, "the woman whose left and right lips do not inhabit the same mouth?"

"You dare not speak that way of my auntie." She was now face to face with him. "...she who has had nothing but your best interest at heart, the woman who went the extra mile to ensure that..."

"Yep, I know...the extra mile, and milked me dry in the process."

"And I don't remember our son having turned out a loser as a result," she added stoically.

"Oh, I see, so the credit for my son's success now rests with your auntie? I thought you had a modicum of decency to attribute that to his step-mother even if you want to obliterate his dad from the picture."

She gave him one of those poisonous looks, and then – just like that - deflated the tension when she added, "For the record, he is my son too."

Kaminata walked in, right through them, as they both acknowledged her inaudible greeting. Then, she turned around, and the three simultaneously cast stares at one another. Just as she attempted to disappear into her room, her mother accosted her, "And where are you coming from this late, young woman?" And, not waiting for a response, she added, "I hope you have not let that fellow who calls himself chairman have his way with you."

"Mother, it's not even dark yet."

"Shut up that beak of yours, my friend. If you dare, I will deal with you, you hear me?"

"Yes, mother." And she turned around to go.

"Come back here, you nonentity; so, did he?"

"Mother, what are you talking about?"

"That long chairman fellow, you chicken brains. Did he try anything foolish with...?"

"Mother, hell no!"

"Yes, hell, that's where you will go if you let yourself fall into his trap."

"I did not even see him today."

"So, because the hunter does not go to the forest for one night, does that stop him from being called a hunter? Look, I keep telling you, you must shine your eyes, my friend. Now, disappear!"

She did.

"You were unnecessarily hard on her," ventured Ekodinge.

"And why don't you let me blow out my fire with my own mouth?"

"Ah, I see, so, this is your little game? I say no to some foolhardy trip and, automatically, I forfeit a say in matters concerning this house?" And he fired on, "Well, since you are bent on staying pick-headed on this one, you tell me just how you plan on getting into Burwandai, woman." He made certain to emphasize woman as if to remind her that, as a woman, it was highly counselled against undertaking a journey of such distance and complexity unaccompanied. Forget the fact that, as far as relations between the two were concerned, both Burwandai and Tobeningo folks slept with one eye open.

The remark from Ekodinge seemed to have jolted her back to sanity; she lowered herself into a seat. Without uttering a word, Ekodinge walked up to her, pulled a seat and sat beside her.

"What did you tell me?"

"What?" answered Scolastica raising her head to look him straight in the eye.

"You would not become wife to your brother-in-law following the passing of ...Zhondezi."

"I don't understand what that has got to do with this."

"A lot, my dear," he answered and continued, "We don't, for a moment, think your brother-in-law will allow you to walk into and out of his trap, do you?" He was playing what the folks here called the politics of bite-and-blow, as she peered into his eyes. By the time he finished piling one reason upon the other to dissuade her, she had the upper part of her body laid on his lap and her eyes shut. When she opened them she called out to her daughter to go into the kitchen and see what she could come up with for dinner.

"And make it quick; it's already very late."

"I did hear everything you told me," she picked up the topic. "But these are desperate times and they demand desperate measures."

"Will you give me some time? I promise I will find a way, like...?"

Raising herself up, she answered, "Like what, dear?" Then she continued, "Alright then, I promise to, but please, don't play the tortoise with this one as time is a luxury we can't afford right now."

They both smiled, and she got up to go hasten things in the kitchen. Just as she stepped out the door, she turned around and apologized for the late dinner. He smiled again. For the second night in a row, the job of hunting could wait. But he would see to it that this night would not wait - or waste.

****

It was not a full week yet after this than Scolastica came up with another scheme. She waited until Ekodinge had gone halfway through his favourite meal, bean pudding cooked in palm oil and served with unripe boiled bananas.

"My dear, I've just received word that my auntie is seriously sick and wants to see me at once. I have to leave in two days' time."

"What? Why not give yourself some more time, say a market week, to prepare? It's not like you've been expecting this, have you?"

Something told Ekodinge he was throwing water on a duck's back; when Scolastica made up her mind about someone or something, it usually stayed that way - for a long time. The sheer shock of this announcement blinded Ekodinge from seeing through her unusual kindness towards him the week before. Or maybe it was the food. This woman was no stranger to the maxim; serve a man his favourite meal and he will in turn deliver even a mountain upon request. Not that he had not commented about this unusual deference earlier. But the woman had smartly covered her tracks then – as now – with, a broad smile, "So, you think because you are not nice to others they cannot or should not be nice to you?" she said. Try as hard as he could, Ekodinge did not get any important details about her aunt's condition that evening.

This was one thing she had never brought up with him. In part it was because she could never put her finger on his pulse on this one. And so, she had kept it all to herself, and, like the meticulous general at war-of-life that she was, quietly going about with her planning. She had, the week before, arranged with the driver of a lorry that traversed Tobeningo every now and then to take food supplies to Motombolombo Government College. Unfortunately, a few days to the appointed date, word reached her that the lorry would not be making the trip. What now? Anyway, better now than at any other time of year, she consoled herself. It was close to Kwanzaa time and a few *spana-nkononis* would, no doubt, be plying through Tobeningo and actually stopping at the local market to scoop up farm produce for faraway towns. All she had to do was make sure she was at the town's road junction early enough in the day. It could take a whole day, or two, but she would find her way out.

And just when she thought this conversation was over, Ekodinge threw in one that almost derailed her, "When you say you have to leave in a few days' time it sounds to me as if this is something planned?"

She quickly recollected herself and countered, "Two days, one day, what does it matter?"

With that, the matter was put to rest.

In an effort to put her mind at rest, she decided she would go confide in her friend the following day. If there was anyone who knew her inside-out it was Enambamu. Enambamu, like Scolastica, was married in Tobeningo but was originally from Burwandai. It was a welcome coincidence as Scolastica had to go help her prepare for her daughter's upcoming *ekekweh* outing and what amounted to an advertising ceremony. It was a proud moment for mother and daughter, and for this her friend since from childhood. She got to Enambamu's just after she was done with market business for the day. The sun was setting lazily, it seemed and soon it would disappear completely behind the majestic Fongetafula, the cue for the animals to begin to find their way back home after a hard day's work fending for themselves in the fields, in the neighbourhoods and just about anywhere they could find sustenance. They chit-chatted on this and that, and then Scolastica broached the subject. They focused on the upcoming rite-of-passage ceremony, she telling her friend how proud she was of her. Her friend intimated her on the post-*ekekweh* program the arrival of the all-female delegation from the bridegroom's family to collect their wife. For now, they had to prepare and decorate her daughter's different clothing items, including beads for the neck, arms, ankles, head and waist to be worn. Then, there were the different dyes and the colouring and decoration of clothing items, earrings and, on the appointed date, the mother of all decorations – her daughter's body.

"A daughter's *ekekweh* is every mother's most cherished dream, my sister."

"Now, you belong to the company of the mothers of the land."

Then, Scolastica dropped the bombshell, and her friend went into an immediate trance, almost.

"*Mungang* what? Are you out of your mind? What business have you – us, children of the most high God – with the ways of Satan?"

"Satan, did you say? What Sango does is not that different from what the reverends do, is it? It strikes me as the height of arrogance to insist that, somehow, one invocation is better – or worse – than the other. They both rely on elements of magic and psychology, if you ask me."

Enambamu clapped her hands, clicked her middle finger and thumb together and with her right hand made a circle above her head. Her sense of incredulity was consummated as she spoke, "Hey, devil, you are a liar, get behind me! May I put it to you that you cannot serve God and Mammon."

"Oh, please, spare me," Scolastica cut in, "and stop taking this thing into the realm of the supernatural."

"Oh yes, supernatural it is as I call on the most high god to wrestle that demon from within you..."

"Oh, shut up your beak, my friend, before...!"

"Before what? Before Epasa Moto strikes me, no, you dead - you were about to say, madam?"

"Lo and behold, if you are not mad, you are sure behaving like one who is."

"For thinking that someone who comes to your home knows which calabash should contain the family oil, I'd say you are the mad one."

"You call me mad, Scola? I say get out of my house, now."

"What? You ask me to leave your home?"

"You heard me right, get out."

Enambamu was about to charge at her friend like an angry bull when a neighbour, in to see what the commotion was all about, stepped in between the combatants.

The neighbour having played the role of peacemaker, left, and the two tried to work out some truce to this bellicose episode. Exchanges, although no less intense, became much more civil.

"I implore you to consider what Reverend Fineglass will say should he get wind of this"

"And how will he get to know?"

"You are asking me? You forget walls have ears, do you" And sometimes, even trees too...and leaves...and rooftops...and..."

"I get the picture," Scolastica lifted her right hand. "But please, just answer me: you are not going to tell him, or anyone else about this, are you?" Her eyes were pleading.

"Me. tell who ? You can rest assured your secrets are safe with me, even when they are dumb secrets," she added, making sure she did not look Scolastica in the eye.

And with that they had ended the duel with none of them able to win over the other.

"Anyway," her friend said, giving Scolastica a hug and a pat on the back, "you know I am your friend – for always. Just want to warn you less it be said tomorrow that I did not discharge my duty toward a sister. Just be careful how you tread"

Noble words. It was true what they said about true friends; they are there to brighten the dark moments in our lives. She smiled, and Scolastica, also smiling, re-assured, "Ah, don't you know me? Of course, I will tread with the utmost care."

It was late when her friend went to see her off. As they walked along the main road – or what they had for one – a vehicle whisked past them raising dust and missing from hitting both women by that much, just as the two uttered a scream and scurried out of the way and into the bush. Scolastica found herself letting out an expletive, before instinctively making the sign of the cross; her friend did same.

"What the heck was that?"

Enambamu answered, "That must be Molekenya, who else? He is the only one with vehicle in these parts, and the only one who drives all the time as if he is high on something."

"Did you call that thing a vehicle?" corrected Scolastica. "To think that he has been using that *spana nkononi* to lure some feather hearts in this town!"

"By the way,' her friend interjected, 'are you still selling your *kwacha* from home?"

"Of course. Why do you ask?"

"Where you not the one who told me the Native Authority had threatened to fine you should you continue to sell from home?"

"Yes, the monster and his agents continue to harass, but you know me, don't you? There is no way I, Scolastica, true daughter of Pa Long Trosa of the proud line of Bandialare, no way am I going to bend for that bastard."

"Scolastica, true daughter of Pa Long, I hear you!" her friend echoed as both women clasped their right palms together and laughed out loud.

There was a moment's pause, then Scolastica added, "Hmh, you know something, my sister?" And before her friend could respond, "I have been thinking, I could bare it all for that fellow."

Enambamu remained silent so her friend inquired, "Did you hear what I said?"

"I heard you, o. Is he not a man and are you not a woman?"

"Tongue, get back in place," she quickly adjusted, and continued, "We have already fought this evening and I don't want us to fight again. But tell me something, my sister, I know business is tough but that does not mean we should give our honour an undeserved bashing?"

"And what do you mean by that?" Scolastica was sounding agitated - again.

She had her arm on her friend's shoulder. "You are a well-respected lady, and this talk of..." Scolastica cut her short, "Come on, what do you think I am talking about? Having an affair with that riff-raff?" And she burst out laughing. Enambamu joined her, still not quite sure why she was laughing.

"Never in my life even if he were the last man standing. The jackass is making my life a living hell and I need to teach him a lesson, that's what I mean."

"How do you mean?"

Scolastica detailed Molekenya's conduct and misconduct, and then asked her pointedly, "How should I go about it?"

Enambamu whispered something to herself; it sounded very much like 'so, this is what this is all about'. Then she spoke up, "Sounds like someone has already decided what to do, well, overkill, if you ask me."

"What?"

"So the nincompoop is pestering you and your daughter and you think the best remedy is to invoke the supreme curse of the land on him the same way our mothers of Burwandai did to the *mukala*? It is against the law of..."

"Did you say law to refer to that outlaw?, Scolastica interrupted yet again"

"You didn't let me finish, Honestly, Scola, if I did not know you well I would say you are a bit edgy. Anyway, I was about to say that would be out of sync with nature's law of proportion. That would be tantamount to attempting to overcome a monkey with an army instead of superior tricks."

Scolastica was not prepared for another fight, so she went along with her friend lecture, and final counsel, "Why don' t we sleep over the matter? With time, they say, every problem gets solved."

"All right, but know that I don't have all the time in the world for that beast of no nation."

They bade each other good night.

Chapter Twelve

The vehicle she boarded was a regular on these roads - or what passed for them. It bore the inscription she thought ominous: *No Condition is Permanent.* True, it was not long since the country had had a measure of internal self-government. But that to her was still no excuse for the generally sore state of the roads in this Native Authority area. It was over two years now, she recalled, when these fellows had come holding boisterous and flamboyant rallies all over the place, cajoling folks, here and there, to join in and vote for them and, in return, promising the sky to every problem raised. Scolastica, never one to put all her eggs in a single basket, had attended rallies for all three main contending camps. Not even such a total spread-out of effort on her part could come to her aid at this moment. Now, she realized how so true it was the warning she oftentimes heard about politicians from her dad - never to take the direction pointed to by any of them. Little wonder their work would soon come to be referred to as *politricks.*

The driver's assistant insisted on and proceeded to collect the full fare from Scolastica and the two other passengers who boarded with her even before their buttocks could come in contact with the solid rough-edged plank pieces that passed for seats. She would have preferred a seat in the driver compartment, something she felt and knew befitted her status as one of the women of substance, a major *buy-am-sell'am,* in these parts. But neither 'first-class' nor 'second-class' compartments had any vacancies.

She immediately announced her colours by insisting on paying only upon arrival at her destination. 'What if this vehicle breaks down before I get to my destination?' was her justification, which was roundly supported by the other passengers. Still, deep down, they all knew it was all water on a duck's back; it was obvious who had the last word in these parts when it came to transporting any kind of cargo.

The driver's assistant, however, had his own rationale why he would not wait until they got to their destinations. He was looking directly at Scolastica as he spoke, "I just want to be certain."

"Want to be certain about what?'

No word from the fellow

"You think passengers will run away with your money, eh, motor-boy?"

Still no utter from the sudden mute, who, after a long silence, suddenly spoke – to no one in particular, "These women, man can never really know what they are up to. In any case, better for me to have my money in my hands first, then, let whatever is to happen, happen."

The opportunity was too good for Scolastica to let slip. "Oh, so, at last, the dumb can speak! What a miracle," she jibbed. Still, she knew they had all lost to these rogues on the roads. Akin to the behaviour of female passengers, and in a resigned mood, she dipped her hand into her bra and took out a small bundle. She untied it with the help of her teeth, pulled out a bill and handed to the assistant. The bill he handed her as change had, from the look of it, seen hard times; it was, as they would say in these parts, a German cargo, a testament to its advanced age and state of dilapidation. An upper corner to it was missing, and it was torn right through the middle. It was held together and assured a continued lease on life thanks to some brownish-looking glue – most likely a plantain extract. That one could barely read what denomination it was, nor much else, mattered little to the motor-boy, who looked only too eager to get rid of it, despite Scolastica's ardent protest for something cleaner.

The distance to Sango Nzogokang's she could do in just about three hours. Today, however, she would be lucky to get there on the same day. From the word go, the Morris lorry-bus was an entertainment mecca with multiple, free-for-all conversations and arguments, all taking place simultaneously. The driver – what a fellow – seemed to be at the origin, centre and tail-end of them all. With a beard the size of a local revolutionary, he puffed on a cigarette, ingested ground tobacco, sipped constantly out of a wrapped bottle he kept under his seat as he joked, cursed and sang in between his tall tales, all at the same time, it seemed. His were tales on every subject under the sun, moon and stars: tales of get-rich-quick opportunities for any lion-hearted, tales of *politricks*, tales of weird customs he had been witness to. And yes, there were plenty of tales of love escapades. He was the most eloquent testimony to the educational force of travel, he asserted, as he repeated, ad nauseaum, names of places near and especially far he said he had been to: Panya – ah, they had the best red wine this side of Planet Earth. He called it Porto, or something of the sort. Next was Jalingombe – where damsels of every taste, size and colour fell head over heels for, and actually over him. And then there was Timbuktu, whose legendary status even Scolastica was not unaware of. Yes, he had been there. To flaunt his credentials, he made sure every song he dished out contained a dose or two of foreign-sounding names:

River Gambia, me noh sabi swim Mami Wata go carry me go River Naija, me noh sabi swim Mami Wata don carry me go

If you marry Lagos lawyer, I don't kia If you marry Timbuktu mallam, I don't kia If you marry Congo hunter, me noh kia If you marry Gabon driver, me noh kia.

No room did he give to the mere mortals he was transporting to question the veracity of his more than outlandish tales. Which was alright by Scolastica, who sat boxed in with her thoughts and could care less about this obvious *garri-boy* of a driver and his motor-boy, who responded to his master's every song, joke and all as if his life depended on it.

With every jerk and swerve of the lorry, her mind wondered to the chairman of the Native Authority; it was obvious the fellow and his types were more interested in their own development than that of ordinary folks. She was eager to get back to base as quickly as possible to begin preparations for Kwanzaa. It was a time that accounted for the bulk of the year's profits for her and everyone else who bought and sold anything for a living.

Then, there was the matter over which she was seeking Sango Nzogokang's intercession; the sooner that was dealt with, the better for everyone. As if her thoughts were not burdensome enough, *No Condition is Permanent* came to an abrupt and screeching stop, this after travelling for less than an hour. The motor-boy, a decrepit fellow whose mouth too had not rested since Scolastica got on, jumped down from the dilapidated truck and proceeded to wedge one set of the rear tires with an oil-dripped and aged piece of mahogany.

"That's it, everybody down, and quickly for that matter. We don't have all the time in the world, now, do we?" He followed his command by actually extending out his arm in a bid to hurry them down; he touched Scolastica on the shoulder.

"You dare not! Get your hands off, you *garri-boy*! Why can't you people fix this damn thing you call a vehicle before you put it on the road?"

As if the cue they had all been waiting for, the other passengers descended with insults on the fellow, who responded with an I-don't-care look, and proceeded to talk to the driver.

The male passengers, as if responding to some military order, immediately lined the edge of the dusty road, facing the bush, each one sending the right arm in between the legs. The women, poor they, had to contend with even more dust and thorny grasses – and the loin-wrap they all seemed to travel with – to hide from any potential prying eyes. Not Scolastica; she squatted right there, not far from the line of men, and did her thing, to looks of consternation from some male and, even more, female passengers. The motor-boy was, by now, under the vehicle, tinkering here and there with his spanner. It was the most indispensable tool, it seemed, in their toolbox – the aptness of the reference, by folks around here, to vehicles in such advanced stage of dilapidation as *spana-nkononi*. His boss leaned, back on the hood, comfortably smoking, snuffing, and sipping from some container hidden inside a small sordid sack. The bottom taken care of, the motor-boy proceeded to open the hood and to test a few things here and there. He came around, had another chat with the driver and then ordered the male passengers to join in and give the vehicle a push and for the women and children to keep walking.

"Just a little difficult stretch ahead of us," he tried to reassure. To more disapprobation from Scolastica, who tried, in vain, to climb back into the vehicle. Just then she felt some warm smelly liquid on her neck. The fowls, goats and pig on the luggage rack above the vehicle were also showing their displeasure, it seemed, perhaps, in reaction to the fact that it had started to drizzle. Scolastica howled and cursed. The motor-boy responded, "You see why it is not good to be head-strong?" She all but massacred him with her eyes. Meanwhile, the motor-boy's 'little stretch' continued to elongate. Just as the pushers were about to give up, the old Morris groaned, shrieked and jerked back to life, dangling from side to side through the narrow, winding road that alternated between rocky hills and rain-filled valleys, thanks to a recent downpour. Scolastica asked the motor-boy if passengers would be reimbursed a portion of the fare for all the help they were giving the operating duo. The sarcasm was greeted with a spontaneous 'yah, that's right, we want a partial refund!' Not a word from either the driver or motor-boy; in fact, the scornful look the latter focused on the source of the remark could kill!

Despite the travails they were going through, it was clear nothing could take away the joie-de-vivre of these folks, as entertaining conversations and even jibes continued to flow from one mouth to the other, old and young alike. She could not tell why at this particular moment but Scolastica recalled having heard that in the *mukala* country free-flowing laughter of this sort was banned, and she wondered how on earth anyone could live in such a place. The woman sitting across from Scolastica pressed her baby's mouth to her left breast. It looked as an attempt not so much to feed as to get the little monster, whose vocal chords had not rested ever since Scolastica boarded the vehicle, to shut up. The baby had barely suckled for a minute than he let it out – prrrrrrr. Many passengers covered their noses. A talkative little boy, on his father's lap – even though the man had paid the full fare for his child – got everyone crazy with laughter when he remarked, in a matter-of-fact way, "Papa, look the trees are running faster than the vehicle! And backwards!"

"Foolish boy," murmured someone, after dutifully taking in on the laughter. Just then the heavens broke open. In fact, the motor-boy barely escaped a good drenching by the time he finished strapping the tarpaulin over the goods and animals on top of the vehicle. This drew a chuckle from the passengers, who fared only slightly better inside.

It was well past daylight when they arrived at a major road junction.

"Who's the one going to that medicine man's place? Come down, here is your stop"

"Looking to do away with an unsteady lover?" mocked someone. A scornful look from Scolastica did not stop everyone from laughing at the remark. She looked out – not that she could identify anything – turned to the passenger to her left, a look of concern on her face. The passenger confirmed and wished her good luck. She alighted and collected her bag from the motor-boy.

"I know the village very well," he said. "Just follow this road, you will go pass a small village and the next big village is his. It is not far at all," he tried to reassure. Scolastica gave him an I-have-heard-that-before kind of look. Just as she bent over to pick up her bag and the vehicle began to crawl on, the motor-boy asked, "Did you pay your full fare?"

"*Garri-boy!*" she shot back.

As she lifted her luggage, she thought she saw a squirrel attempt to cross the road, in front of her! She could not be certain; still, she made the sign of the crucifix – just in case.

****

The atmosphere was quiet – enough to hear a pin drop. It was that kind of night when spirits, good and evil, clearly took over the land, and mortals had to be extra cautious to not cross paths with even the good ones. Even the crickets, bats, owls and other night creatures seemed to lend the cache of the unusual night that hung over Tobeningo and the neighbouring villages. The road that led to Sango Nzogokang's was a pool of muddy puddles. Scolastica walked briskly, turning to look behind her every now and then. Not that she could make out much. That there a strong breeze that got the eucalyptus and other trees going, ruffling their leaves so ever violently, did not help matters. For, if anything, she wanted nothing better now than to have all her body antennas on full alert, including her ability to be able to detect the slightest unusual sound around her. It was not deep into the night yet but the fog, a permanent weather fixture this time of year, contributed to rendering visibility a challenge. She turned on her torch – at intervals – afraid, perhaps, to draw attention to her whereabouts. But if she would not switch it on permanently how was she to know where to place a foot? This, of course, contributed to guaranteeing that she would be knee-deep in mud by the time she got to Sango Nzogokang's. Half-way through a bend, on a steep hill, she ran into a man; a gush of sweat ran down the furrows of her breasts, her armpits and her heart almost leaped from its place. She regained herself, but only slightly, after she saw a woman and a child resting not far from where the man sat. Must be his wife and child, she thought. At least, she had some inward assurance he could not do it in the presence of his wife and, for that matter, a child. A ton of thoughts were running through her mind, including the power of saving grace her people always, and rightfully she determined, accorded to children and women! When she got closer she noticed the woman was eating while the child groaned from obvious pain. The man, in his corner, just sat, his back against a tree trunk, staring into the moonlight that was beginning to pierce its way through the receding fog and the branches of trees. Scolastica offered a greeting, which was warmly responded to. Upon noticing Scolastica, the man had lit his own torch, to reassure both the intruder and himself, maybe. The woman on a mission immediately dropped her bag and slumped to the ground. Yes, she was anxious to get to her destination but there was no way she was going to make it if she did not rest, now; it was a matter of making haste slowly. From the conversation that ensued, she gathered, first and foremost, how much ground she still had ahead of her, that this family was, by some coincidence, returning from consulting the great medicine-man. Sango had sent them away to go procure some essential, and expensive, ingredient to enable the spirits – the good ones – overcome the forces that held sway over their gravely sick child. They exchanged information on their origins, residences and other small talk, Scolastica taking great pains to not divulge the real circumstances and purpose of her trip; if anything, she had been advised to see Sango on account of a gravely ill uncle.

****

A boy - he could be no more than ten, she figured - led her through a series of hamlets and to the back of the compound. Without a word, he beckoned her to a seat, a long wooden bench. She acknowledged the presence of two other occupants to her right, a man and a woman, who returned the courtesy with a nod. Other troubled souls occupied benches facing her and to her left. This sure matches the reputation of the man, the seer, the diviner, she confirmed. The boy disappeared into the dark. The man and woman to her right almost simultaneously fixed a gaze on Scolastica; it was one of those looks that spoke a ton - just as the one the motor-boy had cast on her when she dared to ask for partial refund on her fare. Man and woman both seemed to want to know what business she had showing up at Sango's at such an inclement hour, unaccompanied. Was she one of these women who, finding herself on the wrong side of love, had come to seek some love portion - or worse - for her man? Such stories made the rounds in these parts like water through a basket. With pairs of eyes all in her direction, the otherwise brave woman suddenly developed the urge to urinate. She stepped outside and did her thing - right there in the yard. Making her way back, she accidentally slammed into a container. Some of its contents spilled onto her feet. She took the opportunity to clean if only a tiny portion of the mud off her feet and plastic footwear. The usher came back in and asked the man and the woman to come with him, leaving Scolastica on the bench alone, well, with her thoughts. And thoughts there were a plenty: what if Ekodinge found out about this? What would she tell him? What exactly was she here to find out about? No answers anywhere in the maelstrom of her mind.

Then, in a fast-forward mental switch, she focused on this mystic of a fellow, Sango Nzogokang. What was there to say, or not to say about him? His reputation spread across the width and breadth of the land: from Tobeningo to Burwandai, through Kikaikilaiki, Motombolombo, and beyond. He doubled as a doctor who performed ear-shocking surgical operations such as tearing apart a victim's tibia to repair a broken bone. He dissected stomachs of the dead to extract pieces of evidence of their demise. He functioned with apparent ease in both worlds - of mortals and the spirits. He was even reputed to have singlehandedly come up, in the not-too-distant past, with the magic wand of special broomsticks which his people had used to vanquish the thorny land trespassers from Motombolombo. These were only a handful of the things she had heard about the man she was about to come face to face with. She was still deeply immersed in her own prosecution and life when the errand boy emerged once again, taking her unawares. To her surprise, and relief, this time the boy spoke, "Sango master will see you now."

As soon as they stepped onto the yard something swooped across her face, almost snatching her headscarf with it. From the gushing breeze it left in its wake, she concluded it was some huge bird. Not an owl, definitely not an owl, the spirits forbid, especially since it flew from her left to the right side! She held her breath, made the sign of the crucifix and even genuflected slightly. She wished she had her holy rosary with her, and that she had listened to the counsel of her friend – maybe. She could hardly wait to get back indoors.

The boy was about to enter with her when he noticed she still had her shoes on. With a gesture of the eye, he ordered her to take them off. She immediately jumped right back out, took off her shoes, placing them by the doorway. Then, she stepped back in the most gingerly of fashion into the dimly lit hamlet, as if she expected some sort of reprimand. The boy indicated a corner for her to stand and wait before proceeding to go have an ear to ear with Sango. 'Having an ear-to-ear with seer, but he's just a baby,' she thought, and then concluded with what to her was rock-solid certainty: 'he's his son, being groomed to take over from his Sango, some day.'

Then, he marched right back to Scolastica and whispered into her ear, 'Sango wants to know whether your motive here is to make a mockery of tradition?' Scolastica simply stared at him and then at the old man but did not dare to look him straight into the eye.

'Where is your cock?' the boy inquired. She peered at one corner of the hamlet; cocks and fowls lay in abundance. It was obvious, from the number of fowls, there was not a shortage of distressed souls who had passed by this man for deliverance from the multiple demons of destruction that held sway over their lives – or their minds. When she indicated to the boy she had none, Sango Nzogokang, as if privy to her soul, merely lifted his left hand to indicate his next command. This tiny act was executed with such majesty, lack of effort and even mysticism that Scolastica could only conclude one way: to this being, time, and indeed life, was never meant to be rushed. The boy translated the command to her. She unwrapped her bag, took out her purse, pulled out some bills and dropped in a calabash bowl placed in front of the seer. Then she took a few steps forward towards the corner and sat down. Another non-verbal cue and this time she took position before the seer, squatting unto a stool so low that her knees almost touched her chin. The boy picked the bills, examined and dropped them into the calabash. Then, he looked up above Scolastica's head for a quick moment, and into the bowl. Weird, the weary woman thought. Suddenly, she heard a voice behind her that almost sent her jumping to her feet.

'You had sent word your case was urgent. As you can see, Sango is very busy, so, what about the fee for emergency cases?"

Afraid to look up, she merely responded, "I will arrange for all that tomorrow." Then, she turned to look at Sango once more, and began, "Sango, I have come because..."

"I know why you have come, my daughter," he finally spoke. Okay, judging from the furrows on his face, the bags he carried under his eyes, the grey hair on his head, chin, chest, forearms and even nostrils, Scolastica agreed he was indeed qualified to call her 'daughter.' But she wondered, 'how can he possibly know what is weighing me down?' 'He does not even know me. Well, I have seen him in one other instance – from afar – unrelated to this - but that can hardly mean he knows me. Okay, let's not fuss over this now.'

The boy, as if recovering from a breach in protocol, quickly placed an expansive multi-feathered and multi-coloured headgear on the seer. His headgear adjusted, he took time to stir inside the smoking clay pot in front of him with a long bamboo. He dipped his hand into a small calabash, pulled out a handful of something she struggled to detect. Out of the blue, to Scolastica, he pointed at her headscarf with his bamboo; she promptly took it off, folded and dropped it between her knees. The old man dropped the contents in his hand into the clay pot. Next, he took out cowries from a bag hanging diagonally across his chest and dropped these onto the bare floor. Seven in number. He looked at them intensely, then began, "You are looking for your man."

"Son," she corrected. Or so she thought.

"Man, son, the lion and the tiger can each eat you up, or not?" He did not wait for an answer. Another lesson in protocol for Scolastica! He again picked up the cowries, shook and sprinkled them once more on the floor.

"He is in a faraway place. I see water all around him. And a huge honeycomb on his lap. Not very clear...I also see him on the wings of some huge bird flying over water."

Intrigued, all she could do was ask "Is my son, eh, man safe?"

"Sshh, the Oracle journeys alone and has no need for human legs, not even for basket carriers."

Stare from Scolastica!

"The mouth does not need to direct the fingers how to find it."

He picked up the cowries yet again, shook them in his right palm, sprinkled on the floor and then peered into the pot of water.

"The object of your concern is safe...," he paused, and just before Scolastica could say – or think anything, even – he pursued his thought, "He is safe...a dead man has no problem, no worries; he leaves all that cargo behind for and with us."

"What? hey!" she shouted and placed both hands on the head. She actually attempted to rise but was promptly whisked into staying put.

"Sshh," he ordered again. "The Oracle is not the market."

He was not only a *mungang* but also a diplomat in the art of life; without giving Scolastica any time to amplify her temper, he switched, "Your man, his people are not happy with you. You are keeping something they say is theirs..." And upon the look of disbelief on the face of Scolastica, he added, "...but small matter, the Oracle can stop them."

"Stop them from what, Sango? Is my son, eh man safe?"

He ignored her and peered into the calabash, "What did you do to them that hurts them so bad?"

She did not respond, which allowed the seer to state in a matter-of-fact manner, "But that is not why you came."

"So, that means I cannot go there to try to stop this sacrilege from happening?" She was now deep into defying protocol and it seemed even the seer had decided to let her have her way.

"Ah ha, So, would you like the Oracle to stop them?"

"Yes Sango, yes please...Oracle. I want the Oracle to tell us if I will be safe should I go there?"

"Life owes us nothing; we never want from life. We accept what it dishes." His tone was stern and his look showed he meant it to be that way. "Are your hands clean?"

She was taken aback by the question, and she answered it the only way she understood. "Of course, my hands are clean, Sango. Since when did owing some meagre dowry turn one into a murderer?"

Sango planted an unsettling and bewildered gaze on her. She planted it right back even as her heart was pounding. She knew, at this moment, that she, as her people would say, had arrived. She even allowed herself to wonder - if even for a brief moment only - who or what ever gave old folks the mandate to claim sole ownership of wisdom and matters of that nature. Sango pursued his task, this time throwing the cowries into the clay pot.

"I see a football, it is rolling down a big mountain. You are chasing after it...must catch it before it reaches the foot...a dark lake!"

"Hey, Sango, I, daughter of Naweli, am finished!" She placed both hands on the head, as the other occupants of the room kept their stare. She turned her head around. The voice was still standing there, arms folded across his burly chest. The boy was by the doorway. "Just checking," she fumbled.

"But, but..."

"But what, Sango?"

"Sshh," he lifted his whisk, the tail of some particularly hairy animal, to demand silence. "You must, I say, *must* catch it; if not, you have seen nothing yet. The gods do not take kindly to mortals forcing their hand, not even with a present. You must catch it and keep your present to yourself, do you get me?"

"Yes Sango, but how?" was the feeble response.

"Remember, we do not, I repeat, do not want to offer to the gods what they do not demand of us. If we do that they could just as well forget about that which we seek to present to them – and come after us. Do you hear me?"

She nodded over and over again.

"How, you asked me?"

She nodded again.

"Well, the one who wants to win a wrestling match must enter the ring,"

Back and forth they went until the far into the night. Sango handed her something - she could not tell what it was – and commanded her not to open it on the spot.

The decision of the Oracle confirmed what she had on her mind, the obligation to undertake this mission, to put an end to the pending ceremony.

"You will call their names, seven times each, and rub this against your face before you go," he ordered. "That will take care of the safety, but you must not tempt the gods by presenting them what they do not ask of you; you must wrestle, then."

He waved his whisk to indicate she could take leave. She rose, thanked him with a slight bow and left the room. The boy led her out, picking up her shoes for her.

She requested, and was offered, a place to sleep. It was not much of a sleep as she kept her ears open for the first cock-crow. Meanwhile, she had all the time in the world to play back in her head all that transpired at the session with Sango. From nowhere, the thought of her son engulfed her. What would he think of her? What kind of mother had she been to him if not an irresponsible one?

'Oh dear me,' she suddenly cried out, 'how he was right all along! What will I tell him I have been?' She knew a few of her kind who made a fuss their husbands stayed away from home for extended periods of time because they worked in the *mukala* plantation far away in Motombolombo and could only afford to be with their wives when on some holiday or other. She wanted to rejoice for being in their company, if only for this brief moment, but quickly realized there was neither a consolation in the thought nor any resemblance to the situation of these long-distance marriage types. Ekodinge was bound to get home before her; he always made sure he returned home with the first, or at most the second, cockcrow. She, therefore, still had to prepare a watertight story to tell. Maybe, she had gone to visit and spend the night with her dear friend, Enambamu, who was sick. Yes, that should do it, and, oh, how ingenious! For the first time in a long while, she could afford a smile, uncontrived. With that, she waited, impatiently, for the cock-crow.

Chapter Thirteen

Ekodinge was already home when Scolastica arrived from her trip to the Oracle. She tiptoed in the backyard, fidgeting about the place as she struggled to put her market things in place and with the thought of her on-and-off opponent in her mind. Yes, the 'sick Enambamu' line was a good one, but what if he proved to be smarter, say, by finding out from the girls about her friend? It was as if she had one ear out for a rebuke, grilling or more from Ekodinge. When he heard footsteps in the backyard, Ekodinge called out her name. She came in, they exchanged good mornings and he went back to lying down on the bed. Briefly, she fidgeted in the room and was about to leave when Ekodinge asked, "Are you alright, and are you looking for anything in particular?"

"What makes you think I am not alright?" It was a snap right out of the blue.

He stared at her for a long time and then replied, "Well, because my fevergrass is not ready and you have made no comment about it?"

She hurried out of the room, calling out ~~on~~ for the girls at the same time. He got out of bed, fastened his *sanja* and followed her out to the living room and sat down. She could remain in the kitchen to avoid him, but she had to come to the living room to attend to her market stuffs. He, on his part, made neither a sound nor a move; he merely fixed a stare on her and let the silence do the killing, softly.

"Why don't you just go ahead and tell me that you are suspecting me, or something?" she burst out. Ekodinge stayed on the silence mode. When he decided to speak, it was with the most caustic of facial expressions and tone, "Has anyone heard me utter a word in this house today? Not me, I swear."

****

Even Ekodinge was surprised Scolastica had passed on the shelter provided by the presence in the market to be back home that early that day. Ekodinge picked up his stare from where he had left it in the morning, all the while sipping from a tumbler containing his favourite drink. While he stared, she hurriedly dispatched her two daughters to the farm without much instruction.

"But mom, today is a public holiday, a religious holiday at that," they protested.

"And so what,?" she replied, "Will public holiday come and give us food in this house, pay your school fees, buy your dresses, and take care of...?"

"But it is about to rain, and besides..." they muttered.

"And never you interrupt when I am talking to you," she cut in. "Are you carrying salt on your bodies? How old are you anyway to be afraid of rain? Get out of here, my friends and don't come back to this house without a *kenja* of corn each."

With the girls dispatched, she tried to break the ice once again, "If I didn't know better, I would say you have entered into some secret alliance with some fevergrass deity: it's fevergrass in the morning, fevergrass in the daytime and fevergrass to bathe." Ekodinge did not show the slightest reaction, so she laboured on, "The *kwacha* market is really picking up these days...I wonder what the men of this town are doing with all that *kwacha* they are drinking." She had her eyes on him, and noticed, just then, that the frown had effaced, if only slightly – just like the look she was casting. 'It's tough but I am getting there," she thought.

The girls were back! The stood with pleading eyes, speechless for a while. Then, Kaminata spoke for them, "Uncle, can you please ask her to let us off just for today? My whole body is still aching from yesterday's farm work. Come to think of it, we have been to the farm every day this week."

"Nice try, and will you shut up that dirty beak of yours, my friend," their mother cut her short, as Ekodinge stared at her, the girls, then at her again – speechless. It was Scolastica herself who broke the silence, "Alright, you are off the hook for today; off to the market you go, I will join you later."

Ekodinge was still just sitting there, not doing much, when she disappeared from the living room. When he next saw her, she had changed into her night gown. Gently, she lowered herself onto his laps and began stroking his nose, ears, neck, lips.. She did not need to walk her way down, as she felt his stiff manhood, almost instantly, under her. It was now his turn: "In broad daylight?" She ignored the question and instead threw in a caustic one, "Miracle in the daytime, so, you can talk!"

"And no market today? With whom did you leave your market items?"

"Ah, too many questions," she responded, tapping his lips. "Didn't you hear me ask those heady girls of yours to go to the market?"

Ekodinge looked up at her, speechless; she continued, "And why are you looking at me like that?"

It was the first time he had heard her work to establish any kind of bond between him and the girls – even if heady ones. He felt happy and wished the girls themselves would do same.

She got up and led the way into the bedroom, Ekodinge's *sanja* under her firm grip.

"And what about the windows and doors?"

"Oh, foolish me, where is my head?"

"Between your legs, maybe," he ventured a tease. She did not pay a heed, but released her prisoner and rushed to go shut the windows and doors. She wore a broad grin. It was indeed true what they said about bottom power; it was a force that was slow, silent yet deep and real, below its master and over its slave, a force that always ensured nothing but victory. It was a wonderful victory for they did not finish until mid-afternoon, the gentle rain having arrived and stayed on as the perfect accomplice throughout.

"Good heavens, look at the time!" she shouted, sitting up, sliding her feet into her *samara* and struggling to put on all her wears at the same time. Ekodinge wiped the sweat off his face, neck, armpits and hairy chest.

"What will I tell the girls I have been doing?"

Ekodinge, sitting up, answered, "So, you think they are children, that they don't understand these things or even...?" She gave him a hard look as if to stop him in that line of thought. It was followed by a wry one, and then, "It's all your fault." Then she got up and started to fidget – as far as Ekodinge was concerned – all about the room. When she swung her head around to find his eyes still transfixed on - no, undressing – her, all over again, she inquired, "What, aren't you satisfied?"

"Now, what have I done again?" he answered, as he lifted both hands and placed them on his head. And just before Scolastica could finish I-know-that-look-of-yours, he leapt from the bed and wrapped his hands around her bosom.

"I must go, o, darkness approaches."

He disengaged.

The following day Scolastica had her bags packed. She had reached an understanding, sort of, with Ekodinge on the matter even as she had failed to mention key details about it. As she attended to a few last details, her daughter walked in, uttered a greeting, barely audible, and dropped her market bag and basket.

"What's the matter, now, Kaminata?" her mother asked, a look of concern on her face, before firing away, "Why do you look like the Fongetafula on your back this time? It's that chair fellow again, eh... What does the dog want... Kaminata, are you pregnant?"

"The spirits forbid!" a suddenly re-energized Kaminata screamed, clucking all her fingers over her head. "Mom how can you even think such a thing?" An unapologetic Scolastica merely added, "You can't blame a mother for worrying over her daughter's welfare, can you? You know you are now a young, beautiful, fully developed woman and the envy of this town. You must beware of the sharks who walk about disguised as men." Then, she immediately switched the subject, "In fact, someone has to do something about this he-goat; his case is becoming one big nuisance for this town."

With that, she moved over to take a look at the bread baking in the oven. She stoked some firewood into the fire on and underneath the oven. Just then, a lanky fellow walked into the yard. Scolastica immediately recognized him as one of Molekaya's acolytes and accosted him.

"What do you want?" she screamed.

"Eh, I am looking for one big girl who lives in the compound," the fellow answered.

"One big girl who lives in the compound," Scolastica shot back in the most sarcastic of mimicry she had ever found herself produce. In this town, the womenfolk had elevated this into an art form, and there was little doubt who the queen of them all was. Her peers often teased and wondered why there was no silver cup for sarcasm – they were sure who its perpetual winner would be.

"Go tell whomever that sent you that you have not found the house."

"But my investigations have led me to confirm that this is where she lives," he countered.

"Eh eh, your investigations... I tell you what...you are right." "Kaminata!" she called out, unexpectedly, even for the messenger.

"Mother, did you call...what's going on here?"

She lifted her hand to call for silence, and addressed the stranger, "Here she is, and I will get her ready for you, if you give me a moment." Kaminata put both palms over her mouth; her mother raised her hand a second time. "You go back in there and get ready," she ordered her.

The man, perplexed, answered, "But madam. I was not asked to take her anywhere; I just have a special delivery for her."

"From whom?"

"Eh, from....from Mister Molekaya."

"I see, the chairman, why did you not say so? Please, have a seat."

The next thing anyone saw was a furious Scolastica, her loin-wrap firmly girded around her *kabba*, dishing out the traditional treatment at the fleeing messenger, who hit a tree stomp and fell, but got back on his feet before it was too late. Scolastica called out at her daughter to put another pot of water on the fire

This chairman must be that spoke in her wheel, after all, that the oracle – or was it Sango - had talked about. Yes, he had said 'I see you on a bicycle, riding, up the hill. I see a man

120

holding a heavy stone; he is trying to fit it in between the spokes of the bicycle.' Words to that effect.

****

The chairman of Tobeningo Native Authority area was a tall, charcoal-dark fellow with a pair of cicatrices on each cheek. He had sunken eyes. He wore a long moustache that descended past both sides of the lips, a delight it was to watch every time he settled down to consume *kwacha* or some other foamy substance! His receding fore-hair would not have been of any significance but for the company he loved to keep – sweet-sixteens. The chairman drove a retired Morris no one was sure for certain how he acquired, although many could bet their hunch they did. He had bought it from the departing manager of the nearby coffee plantation. He had a legion of errand boys at his beck and call. The only thing he seemed to enjoy doing by himself was working on his *spana-nkononi*; this he did on a daily basis, almost and with the utmost delight on his face. That he spent more time fixing - or attempting to fix - the thing than actually riding it was of no significance. From the stories of his escapades, it was hard to tell which one between the vehicle and him gave the other more trouble. He was a talk of the town but by no means a toast of the town. One of his parents, it was widely advanced, was from Kikaikilaiki, which was hated with passion in Burwandai. It was widely believed its people had worked in tandem with the *mukala* to conquer and run roughshod all over the people of Burwandai, Tobeningo, Motombolombo and the rest of the Authority area. Still, he had his own share of admirers, or bootlickers, depending on whom one talked to.

The man too bore a few grudges against Scolastica and her family. Many years earlier, her father had stepped in to separate a cutlass fight between this man's uncle and a heavy debtor neighbour just as his uncle was about to land the fatal slash. That Scolastica's father had received a serious cut in the arm from the uncle's cutlass meant nothing to the chairman fellow; he continued to blame her father for making his uncle spend several years in jail for nothing. If only his uncle had been able to finish the job…! His grudge against Scolastica and her family, then, was a question of honour. But it was honour that was severely compromised by his own desires for the flesh, with Scolastica's daughter being only one in a line of sweet-sixteens he seemed to have solemnly swore before some altar to conquer.

Scolastica walked briskly, dragging her grown-up daughter by the arm as if she were some sheep being led to the slaughter. Her *kabba*, tightly girded by a loin-wrap around her waist, swept the street in a rhythmic left-right movement. It was a long walk across town. Some little boys, sensing something juicy, began to trail the pair as Scolastica divided her time between cursing whomever and whatever, haranguing her daughter and just plain talking to herself. Meanwhile, the dust continued to rise behind them and, in front of them, the sheep, goats, fowls, pigs, dogs to scatter.

"I swear you this child will kill me before my time."

"But mother, I have done nothing wrong. Is it my fault that I am pretty?"

"Oh, shut up that stinking beak of yours before I shut it off permanently. So you are pretty, but does that give you the right to conduct yourself as if you are some open shop inviting every buyer to come inside. I have always warned you about those short tights you call dresses. And you think I have not been watching how you have become best friends with rain? With no bra on, I might add. Remember, you chicken head, that I too have been a girl before. A calabash that is noisy will never be used to carry the family oil." She gave absolutely no room for Kaminata to put in any word.

When they arrived, they found the chairman under the hood of his vehicle, and with a spanner, fidgeting here and there on the engine. No surprise there; between this thing and sweet-sixteens it was hard to tell which he loved more. Scolastica gave him no time to finish his greeting before launching into her tirade. It was not the first altercation between them. On several previous occasions, she had accosted him over unpaid bills; somehow, she had been under the mistaken impression that a man so into the habit of wanting to please anything in a bra, would mind a lot about his public image by staying away from debts and the public embarrassment that often trailed it. Today's encounter was different; she would no longer be civil toward the he-goat, not after the brazen manner he and his acolytes had begun to approach his daughter. This woman was determined no way was Kaminata going to end up the way she did. Unfortunately, it seemed, every part of Kaminata's busting and bubbling anatomy was bent on defying a mother's sacred dreams for her daughter.

"You old shameless he-goat, why can't you find someone your age or better still, keep to your so-called wives?" He did not respond, which infuriated Scolastica even more.

"I am talking to you, he-goat, who chases anything in a bra in this town."

"Mother, please..." Kaminata tried, not so much to stop her as to have her keep her tone down.

"Shut up, my friend," mother screamed at daughter, "and don't be stupid. For whom am I doing this? This is how you allow beasts of no nation as this one here take advantage of you...just because he can drive some, some..." She raised her voice even higher, giggled and pointed at the object of her derision, "The dog calls this *spana-nkononi* a vehicle."

"You nincompoop, enough, and watch your dirty mouth. Do you know who you are talking to?" he shot back. She mimicked his question in the most sarcastic of tones before adding, "Stinking mouth, you too."

"Woman, do you know I can have you arrested?"

"Me, you have me arrested....what for?"

"For bringing public authority to ridicule....and for trespassing," he quickly added, apparently realizing the tenuousness of the first proposition.

Scolastica clapped her hands, smiled, and pointed at him, "This banana stick will have me arrested for ridiculing public authority, ha, ha. If only there was a public authority anywhere in the horizon. My people, does anyone see any authority around here? I see only a dog that cannot keep the tentacle in between its thighs in check."

Keeping his cool, he tried to re-adjust his shot and deflect her charge, "Remember, I have a file this thick on you." He lifted both hands and formed an imaginary ball to demonstrate just how big this file was. "From fomenting illegal strikes, engaging in witchcraft to weapons-running – need I continue?" That seemed to prick Scolastica, who remained quiet – for a long while. Just as a curious bunch of onlookers – some with *kenja*s of cargo for the market on their heads - began to form. Their world could run all it wished around them but these folks were not ones to let that carry them along; there was almost a moment to stand and stare and laugh at our own human pleasantries, even foibles. And the kids were catching up to it fast. Standing with the bunch was an excited group of little boys who had trailed mother and daughter all the way from the far side of town. Everyone was having a field day.

"What did I just hear you say?" one of Molekaya's wives, who was stepping out to head for the market square, joined the fray. "Oh, you have finished tasting all the men in this town and that's not enough for you, swine; now, you've decided to focus your claws on my husband, eh, *ashawo*?"

"Not even if this goat were the last one standing," Scolastica shot back as the woman swiftly ran her bellicose gaze on Scolastica, Kaminata, then on her husband. Just as she tried to repeat the act, Scolastica charged at her with all her ferocity and venom of an angry woman. Her daughter joined in. Before Molekaya could decide to join in – in an apparent bid to free his wife – Scolastica had grabbed her by both legs, wrapped her thighs together and flung her to the ground. Both mother and daughter turned her into a punching bag, feeding her dust and grass in the process.

****

There she sat, in the middle row, arms crossed and her friend by her side. It had been a long wait so far; if they were outside, they would not have seen their shadow. This affair was so stealing into her time she had even toyed with the idea of escaping the court date and making it to Burwandai at once. But she had been counselled out of the idea by her friend Enambamu.

Then she jumped to her feet as her friend promptly pulled her back down with a reprimand, "What is the matter with you?"

"Is that not my name I just heard?"

"Are you dreaming? Yes, you must be dreaming."

They would have to wait some more. For now, there was another defendant in the dock.

"Woman, can you state your name for the court?"

There was an unmistakable aura of authority in the voice and the manner the question was asked. She answered, and the usher proceeded to the next question.

"What is your residential address?"

'Strangers Quarters, Tobeningo," she obliged.

"And what is your profession?"

The woman toured the jam-packed make-shift courtroom with her unsettling eyes. Her voice dropped just one notch as she replied, "Ah di waka, sah."

"Speak up so that this honourable court can hear you. I say, where do you work?"

"*Ah di waka, sah.*"

"*Ah di waka,*" he repeated mockingly, before adding, "Can you tell this honourable court what you mean by that, and do not waste the time of this honourable court, woman."

The judge summoned the usher to the bench. His attention was drawn to something; when the judge resumed the questioning himself, it was evident what that was. It was clear the *mukala* had left an indelible, if not *honourable*, impression on this one!

"Woman, what do you mean by '*ah di waka*'?

The woman was flabbergasted, "Ah ah, is there anyone here who does not know what I mean?"

The courtroom burst into a unanimous laughter.

As if on cue, both judge and usher shot up simultaneously, each his own way.

"Shut up, my friend," the judge fired and banged his gavel on his bench.

"Order! I say, order!" the usher screamed wildly, suppressing any further amusement the crowd was getting out of this.

The disorder quelled, the three-pronged charge of loitering on public property with no reason, illegal solicitation and engaging in a proscribed trade was hurriedly read and slammed against the occupant of the dock. As she stood down, the hypocrisy of this kind of justice could not be more obvious: here were the men who by night courted her for her services now condemning her by day for offering the same service.

Scolastica's case was no different. The verdict was a swift one: assault, defamation of character and breach of public order and attempted possession of a proscribed weapon. How she escaped a charge of procurement of a proscribed weapon, she herself could not fathom. Perhaps, it was one of these charges which, as her people always maintained, its authors could not dare advance for fear it would bring even them down with the victim. As she stood down from the dock, she instantly remembered a comment her father used to make on the weirdness of the *mukala*'s justice. Here she was, being found guilty while a chronic debtor and molester was going scot-free. Forget the fact that she escaped a lock-up on a technicality, her statue as woman of substance publicly recognized and coming to her rescue, and after she opted for the option of paying a fine. Still, it was some justice, indeed.

As always, whenever in tight situations like this, her mind shifted to something else, usually one equally daunting. Then her mind shifted to Ekodinge; he must be in by now. She had not let him in at all on her run-in with the chairman and she was confident the man's own precarious living would not allow him the slightest opportunity to get wind of this – except, of course, the president of the fraternity of drunkards happened to trespass into her own compound. Now, she had to race against time if she espoused the slightest hope of averting disaster from taking place in Burwandai. She found one saving grace in the fact she was no longer on a war path with Ekodinge over this trip. After all, she was going to visit her sick auntie. To his question as to what she would do if her late husband's brother found out about her presence in Burwandai, she had answered, smiling, 'I am not going for some empire day parade, am I? Of course, I am going to keep a low profile, stay indoors and if all that is not enough, what if I wore a disguise – like grow a moustache or something – during my time over there? Would that be enough precaution for you?'

She had done everything she could think of to cover her tracks. She had worked on her daughters, pleading with and then warning them of the consequences of Ekodinge finding out. She did not give them all the details either but she could see they were visibly disturbed.

****

Through her extensive network, she had got wind of her son's impending arrival. In fact, according to one of her sources, her son was already in Burwandai, or thereabout, now almost a year since the disappearance of his father, declared killed during a hunting expedition under circumstances that had still to be elucidated. It was time for the spirits to be appeased, for him to be declared of the after-world through a public commemoration during which the son would be publicly declared his successor. Scolastica was furious; the case against her had delayed her departure. But for it, she surely would be in Burwandai by now. She suddenly realized she had let up on other vital areas of her preparation. She was so into wanting to nail the proper look and sound that she had, over the last little while, forgotten to restrict her rehearsals to private quarters and moments.

"Scolastica!,' Ekodinge shouted one evening when he caught her rehearsing, 'how many times have I called you?"

"I'm sorry, I did not hear you."

"Of course, how could you when you were busy reciting I-don't-know-what? What was that, anyway?"

"What? Nothing, I was merely thinking aloud..."

"Thinking aloud over what?"

"Ah, ah, why all these questions? Was thinking how sluggish business has crawled, is that okay for you?"

He did not say anything but she knew that, deep down, he did not believe her one iota.

Chapter Fourteen

They arrived just as the sun was going to sleep behind the Burwandai hills. They passed several compounds before Ekodinge's. Scolastica instantly recognized several of them including that of the brother she refused to marry following the death of her husband. It was a defiance that had led to a level of notoriety, and certain folk-hero status among a coterie of maidens just about to enter into or graduate from *ekekweh*. If only these knew the heroine of theirs, who was already in song, was now entering their town, blood and flesh, bones and soul! Tears ran down her cheeks and into her beard as her eyes fell upon her husband's tomb. A pang of tension seized her as she found herself overcome by emotion. Her nipples hardened inside her thick clothing. Her pace slackened. Starring at the tomb, she began to wish she could take if only a brief moment to fulfil just one tiny end of a string of spousal duties she suddenly found herself sorely missing – like planting flowers and removing the weeds. Her travelling companions, observing her distressed state, discharged her of her bag for the remainder of the trek.

****

Ekodinge's compound was packed; people had come from all over for the ceremony. You could tell from the costumes of the many of the menfolk, Ekodinge was considered a man of timbre and calibre. Ganchu was dressed in the skin of a crocodile, his father's famed insignia. The procession was now in the centre of the grounds. Someone presented a rifle to the chief celebrant; Ganchu pointed it to

131

the sky and released its content to the ululations of the womenfolk and nods of approval from the titled menfolk. A man danced to the front of the procession as if to engage Ganchu in a dance. Then he whispered something into Ganchu's ear and vanished just as swiftly as he came. Ganchu continued to execute dance steps in the procession. The messenger appeared again ad this time tapped him hard on the shoulder.

"What, can't you see I am about to...?"

The messenger pleaded with his eyes as if to say 'not here, please' while indicating with the right hand what he wanted done. Ganchu obliged, and was being led away when Emerald, taking in the ceremony from a canopy of palm fronds with a camera that would not stop clicking, stood and approached the pair as they made their way to the backyard.

"Honey, where to?" She turned to the messenger, "Could you please excuse us, I would like to talk to my husband, in private." She pulled him by the arm, away from the messenger. When they were alone, she asked to go with him but he turned it down. As he walked back to re-join the messenger, she pulled him toward her open chest and planted a long lip-to-lip kiss. The crowd looked on, some giggling, others stupefied. Away from the crowd, Ganchu asked the messenger, "What's going on?"

He replied, "Be patient, brother, there are some men, they say have trekked from afar and would like to have a word with you."

"Well then, who are they and where are they? I have a village out there and a ceremony to kick-start. Some aspect of the ceremony no one told me about, maybe?" He smiled at what he thought was his quick thinking. The messenger too smiled and nodded.

"Ah, then you should have said so." Again, he smiled and looked at the messenger as if for some approval. Again, the man fit to be his elder brother by several moon-cycles, showed a pair of kola-reddened teeth that immediately turned into a grin as if to let Ganchu know to whom and from whom customary hierarchy demanded deference.

While the messenger had been gone, Scolastica was busy making sure everything was still intact in the disguise department. Her mind began to wander between her assignment, her home and man in Tobeningo, and the altercation, only recently, with her daughter. And the clay-like stone Sango had given her? Ah, good, it was firmly in place. She quickly pulled off the chain from around her neck, and seven times each, she called the names of those she wanted neutralized – for the reasons the Oracle had advanced. Then, she spat on the nod twice and threw the chain back on her neck.

The messenger tapped on the door. Scolastica peeped through a crack, and opened. As she stepped into the room, Ganchu rose to his feet. She ran toward him, arms outstretched, and forcing Ganchu to, reluctantly outstretch his in response. But she stopped dead in her tracks; not now, she reckoned, as the situation was still dicey. Besides, the elements on her chest were bound to give her away in a warm embrace. Ganchu was hit by the eyes.

"Oh my...how I am glad and blessed to see you." By Jove, she almost did it again; it was becoming obvious she had not done flawless job on the voice front. It was obvious she was being overcome by the natural instincts of a mother. That made Ganchu pull back, as he hit the stool with a heel, losing his balance. He was up in a heartbeat. Briefly, he turned and glanced at the messenger as if to charge him for bringing him in here. Then, the focus was back on this man. Well, he figured, it was not inconceivable, although the odds were astronomically against it, to come across a man the vocal timbre of a woman. In this land, where talk was like the air they breathed, the lazy and careless tongues always held that such men went with other men. He struggled to forbid his mind from going further down this path. The one in front of him was bearded – very much so. He turned again to look at the closed door. Then, he addressed the man, this time in an animated tone, "The number of grey hairs on your head and face bestows on you the right to be addressed and on me the obligation to call you father. Now, father, what is this all about? Even more important, you have not told me who you are."

"For those kind words may the spirits of this land be with you and may the ground on which you walk always be soft under your feet," was the reply. And then, "Who or what I am must take a backseat to what you are about to do."

'What I am? What are you...?' But he did not ask that. Instead, he asked, timidly, "What is it that I am about to do?"

"Commit a crime against the land, and the spirits, and Epasa Moto," and as if for emphasis, categorically added, "and not even Obasinjom can fault me on this one." There was a long pause as everyone present looked around and at one another. When Ganchu broke it, it was with an enraged tone,

"Now look, I don't know what this is all about, and frankly, I could care less; whatever it is, it has to wait. The spirits of my father, bless his soul, will be enraged, and worse, if I do not return out there now and carry on with this ceremony as custom demands." And with that he turned to make for the exit.

"That is what I came to talk to you about, my son." It was like some demon she had finally cast out of her, but she was still not sure if the time was ripe. "And by the way, you solemnly promise not to even think of resuming this thing until I have left town, for I do not entirely expect petals to be thrown at my path here."

Yet again, he faced her, slowly, and this time, she was on her knees. That he had been addressed 'son' he did not find unusual, for what child of Burwandai was not a son or a daughter before any adult? After all, did the good folks here not live by the code which maintained it takes the whole village to raise a child, and that a woman's child is hers only in the womb?

"Please, in the name of the living-dead of Burwandai and Tobeningo, in the name of the line of Bandialare, you must hear me out, Kikiriki, I speak the truth. I have come to tell you the whole truth." Okay, who did not know about his dad and his exploits? But Kikiriki? As far as he could recall, only his grandmother on his mother's side had ever called him by this name. Whoever was in front of him right at this moment must know something about his grandmother. What was that thing, what was their relationship, if any, and better still, who was this? And what truth was he talking about?

"First, and I am forced to repeat myself,' she continued, 'you have to, please, put a stop to what is going on outside there; it is not right."

"What do you mean?" he inquired.

"Please, sit down, Kiki....this is what happened."

Scolastica looked at the messenger and, as if on cue, he exchanged places with a small group of elderly men. Still standing outside, one of them called out, 'Ganchu, are you there? The chief will soon be here to perform the ceremony.'

"That is what I want to talk to you about."

"You've said that more than once."

Scolastica had barely started to make her point than the door was flung open. A red-faced Emerald shoved herself into the room. Toeing her were two elders, who stepped in one after the other and at once huddled to one corner.

"Honey, what in hell's name is going on?"

"Woman, is this how they intrude where you come from?," an elder quizzed the intruder. The others, however, seemed to have been jostled by a surge of electricity as he rubbed his eyes to take a closer look at her. Both women stared at each other, almost motionless, with Scolastica exerting extra effort to examine this foreigner. From top to toe, from side to side, and from boobs to backside, she examined. It was as if Emerald's extra frame at both the front and back ends was in the way of her all-important assessment. Emerald showed a clean pair of teeth, but that did not impress Scolastica. Neither did the hand she stretched out; the gesture was over even before it began as the generalized stare forced her to bring her hand back to its original position. The intensity of the mother's stare seemed to say one thing, 'my son, do you want to tell your mother this is the best you could come up with in the *mukala*'s country, this *dakifankwo*?' Then aloud, she fired one of those bullets that had come to define her character, "I wonder how people ever get to do anything – or even think – in that land you come from, son, when they are always talking when not talked to." This was followed by another awkward silent moment, broken, as always, it seemed, by Scolastica.

"As I was about to say before the rude interruption, this kind of celebration is for someone who has journeyed to the land of the immortals; it is not for you to perform."

"Can you, for one moment, please be specific?"

"He has not joined the company of his ancestors."

"How can you be so sure? You never lived with my father, and now you want to play judge over his character and god over his fate?" His tone was brash and startled even him. Not giving up, she again made for his ear – not before she had indicated to the elders and Emerald to leave them alone – "Your father is alive, and this you promise not to tell anyone...I mean, no one whatsoever."

"Of course, he is. Who in this land questions the unity that exists between the worlds of our departed beloved and ours?"

"Shut up my friend and listen to me. Your dad is not dead; that means he is alive. Did you hear me? He is alive - and I know where you can find him. With me!" She blurted out the whisper, thumping her chest for emphasis and credibility. Another proof she was, indeed, someone with a deep connection not only to his grandmother this time, but to him, Ganchu. She had, in her excitement, given away her identity through her voice, and for the first time, Ganchu put the pieces together.

"Mo -, mo- mother?," he stammered.

"Ganchu, what the heck...?" Emerald ventured but was immediately forced to cover her mouth with her hand as soon as a powerful "sshh" was directed her way by the master of the moment. Not even bothering to look at the object of her scorn, Scolastica added, mockingly, "always this inattentive?" Emerald, who had stood defiant – and had ignored signals to vacate the room- watched in awe as Ganchu ran into his mother's warm embrace. Mother and son basked in each other's warmth even as the tears began to flow, freely. Just then, the two elders she had sent out, made their way back into the room. They stood in one corner, heads locked together, and although they spoke only in whispers, something in their mannerism caught Scolastica's attention. It would be better if Chief Lohkoh-Lohkoh knew about this before he made it to the ceremonial grounds – if only to avert a calamity of a different kind, but a calamity, nonetheless, they seemed to be saying. She decided to finish their thought for them.

"So ..." Wrong voice!

"So, is anyone heading to the palace to take care of things, or are we all just going to stick around and stare at I – don't-know-what?"

"And who do we say is the bearer of this loaded kenja?" one of the elders asked. As they pondered their response, it was left to the messengers bearing the horn and the gong to draw their attention to what was happening in the yard. Unless their ears were playing tricks on them, a protocol breach was in the process of being committed. The two elders burst out of the room. As soon as they left, Scolastica excused herself, jumped into an adjacent room, but was back out in no time.

"I swear, son, I swear I owe you a complete explanation – afterwards!"

Before anyone could react, she was making her way into the ceremonial grounds. She was well on her way when she turned around, as if to ascertain the correctness of her move, and asked "are you coming or will you just stand there like a pillar and stare at me?"

She ran toward the gong messenger and exchanged talk with him, ear to ear. The messenger showed a clean pair of heels and caught up with the two elders heading to the chief's palace. Still confident in her disguise, she squeezed her way through the huge human circle. Now, what? Stop the music and the gaiety that was going along with it, and then say or do what? Her heart was beating faster than her head could think, to which her body responded as if on adrenaline, or worse.

She engaged a small group of women dancers and led them, shoulders quivering at a frenetic pace, face to face with the drummers in the centre of the huge circle. She danced and danced, swirling round and round, her captives obliging and matching her every move. Scolastica raised one hand and leg into the air, spun around, and as if to step onto the central drummer's set, brought the drumming to a sudden stop. A few ululations from a handful of women. Hers had not been any moves to write home about; in fact, they drew raised eyebrows, finger-pointing and other manners of disapproval from many in the crowd, for whom this man stuck out like a sore thumb. What is more, he had preferred to dance heavily clothed, not to say, wrapped up - in such boiling weather!

"Some kind of *segele*," summed up a septuagenarian, leaning heavily on a third leg, before adding, "The spirits of my forebears protect our culture when I am gone, else...!" Even without being privy to the damning evaluation of her performance, Scolastica's mind, in a fleeting moment, went back to the years of her youth when she paid heed to anything but learning and participating in the songs and dances of her people. But regret could come later; for now, the energized robot in her had some serious business to accomplish.

"People of our land, I salute you; you are a great people."

"Yeah," went the chorus.

"You are number one in the entire Native Authority area."

"Excellent talk."

"No one will ever mess with you."

"Never!"

"My fathers and mothers, if we continue to stand tall it is all because we stand on the sturdy shoulders of you who have come before us. I am a close friend to your son here." She turned around to look at Ganchu. Not immediately catching any glimpse of him, she went on, "I mean the one on whose honour we are all gathered here tonight. I represent an important organization in the *mukala*'s country in this whole Native Authority area and beyond. Through your illustrious son, we have heard about the many problems besetting this locality. As a matter of fact, he singlehandedly prepared and sent us a request for assistance. And I am proud to say that the *mukala* organization I represent, after careful examination – mind you, we received hundreds of such requests from all over the world – is prepared to give the request a favourable reply." She made another futile attempt at drying the river running down her forehead as the crowd clapped at her sweet words.

"And who did you say you are, again?" a voice from the crowd shot out, before pursuing, "And which is your family compound?" Totally unexpected, the question produced more sweat; not that it mattered. First, she re-adjusted her pitch, which had begun to show signs of faltering. Then, she lied; she said everything but the fact that she was actually from Burwandai, and that she, actually, had a few skeletons in her closet regarding Burwandai. As she spoke, her eyes actually caught those of her late husband's brother. With the speed of lightning, she turned to face the crowd to her back. Never mind the fact this solution created a serious breach in protocol; she now had the men of timbre and calibre to her back!

"And how come, my son, that his Highness is not made aware of the presence of such an august visitor?" The same fellow as before – 'indeed, some people are put on this earth to cause trouble for others. Or, maybe this fellow has actually made me out,' she thought. The question might have been addressed to Ganchu who had, unnoticed to his mother, made his way to join her in the centre of the circle. Yet, it was Scolastica who felt the earth move under her feet – if only it would open and swallow her up and put an end to her misery. Better to die this way than through the mob justice that was sure to follow, she figured. She decided to face up to her demons. Once again facing the men of timbre and calibre, she responded, "My most esteemed elders, our people say that when a child is learning how to play the drums he does not do so on the day the chief is taking a new bride. As I speak to you, there is another high-powered delegation at the palace briefing his majesty; that explains why the Conquering Elephant is not here yet. I mean, would you rather he forgot about that high-powered delegation from the city and the *mukala* country to be with us here?"

"A curse," a voice rang out, as Scolastica sought to dive and hide, only for the voice to add, "that would be a curse." She tapped Ganchu on the shoulders, just as a group of elders, each with a third leg, got up and began to hurry, in their own way, out of the compound. Emerald adjusted her camera. Ganchu dived and got the flash straight into his face – just in time! There was a collective sigh of relief from the crowd. Scolastica peered at Emerald, and would have unleashed her venom at her but for the spot in which she now found herself. She would take care of her later; the departing elders were, for now, a bigger fish on her frying pan.

"His majesty in an earlier audience he granted me, commanded that, on no account whatsoever, should he and the delegation be disturbed," she announced publicly. And turning to Ganchu, she ordered "that's what you must tell those two; now, move!" Ganchu raced after the men. It was a real treat seeing Emerald as she fought to go after Ganchu;

this exercise could, conceivably, last her a moon-cycle! Many folks simply shook their heads.

"Now, as I was saying, resumed Scolastica, 'inasmuch as this is an important tradition that was about to take place here today – and it must be honoured, you hear me , my people? – it must be honoured, but for now, it has to wait. For long, Burwanda has been struggling for an identity; are you a small town or a big village? Look at the others, and I shall not call names here tonight because you all know them. Electricity, water through pipes – you too can have these, and more. And with them stamp on a solid identity for Burwandai in these parts. For, what is about to happen to Burwandai is something that happens only once in a lifetime. It is such a golden opportunity that, should you let it slip by, hmh, or, did you want to?"

"No way," was the general response.

As long as the words kept on coming she would keep on speaking – and so she did. As she spoke, she kept a watchful eye in the direction Ganchu and the elders had taken. The three were standing under a kolanut tree and engaged in what appeared to be a heated discussion. 'I have to find a way to get out of this ordeal, *now*,' she affirmed to herself. But then, a lie, once told, tends to look for another lie to cover it, and so on and on she piled them. She told the crowd the organization 'he' represented had sent 'him' to come get Ganchu right away and over to the city to meet a delegation from *mukala* country to conclude some very important negotiations concerning the request he had put on behalf of Burwandai.

"You mean the *mukala* has actually sent some of theirs over here for this?" a fresh voice from the crowd questioned.

"That's correct."

"How come they are not here?"

"Ah, ah, am I not their colleague, and is your son not their friend, one who has dined, played, speaks their language and does many other things with them? You don't ask for the father to confirm his son, do you?"

"Of course not," the crowd shouted.

"By the way, if your voice is giving up on you, mister, why don't you ask to smoothe your throat with some of our first-grade palm wine before you return to the *mukala* to say we did not treat you well?" The crowd was now firing from all cylinders. The costumes on her body were weighing her down. Why in the name of the spirits did she insist on cooking up this hanky-panky of a trip even in the face of repeated vetoes? What kind of mea culpa – if it could be called such – was it, even on behalf of a son she loved dearly, if it meant death? But if not this, what else? She was going berserk. It was then that Zhondezi's brother, seeing how drenched this 'man' was, hollered, "I hear it is pretty cold where you come from. But if you have not noticed, it is hot here, though, and we don't dress as if...here, why don't you take off some of that heavy clothing that is obviously weighing you down?"

'Oh spirits of the land, it's this man, and he actually wants to come get me - right here!'

"No, no, no," she shouted at both the man - and at herself, half-shutting her eyes. 'Gosh, these *mami wata* eyes of mine!' Taken aback, the man froze in his tracks, momentarily twisting his face as Scolastica held out both hands to indicate No trespassing. She felt the earth move under her feet – yet again – as this man regained his confidence and continued his stride toward the centre of the ring. 'Gosh, these devilish eyes of mine!' Should she shut them? 'If only this earth would please, open up your bowels – *now I say* – and take me, and put an end to this misery,' she pleaded – and immediately collapsed. Ganchu, back from his meeting with the messenger-elders, Emerald and her carriers ran up to her and formed a human circle around her. Some in the crowd surged forward to get a better view; others recoiled in horror and many gave our shriek cries of fright. Scolastica was gasping for air. Take the protective layers off this leopard, or what? It was left to Ganchu to worry about this

Before she knew it, she was clutching Emerald by the arm and pleading with her for the umpteenth time, "Hold on just a little bit longer, we shall soon get to this small village, right after we cross a stream and go up a small hill – not far from here, really, and there we can rest for the night, if you prefer."

'What other night is this woman talking about,' thought Emerald. If truth be told, it was now nearing dawn. It was a cold yet bright night, and the moon and the stars were out in full force. For substantial stretches of their arduous trek across the open grass fields, they could not only see their shadows but had not had no need for their torches.

Ganchu, sweating under the weight of his own *kenja*, could not be of much assistance. Still, looking at Emerald, he could afford to smile every once in a while as if to say, 'I told you not to come but you would not listen.' But to his mother; it was much serious business, such as "Mother, how could you tell the crowd that chief had asked not be disturbed even after the gong and horn had announced his arrival for the ceremony?'

"Well, the gong and horn announcement simply said someone important, who said it had to be the chief, eh? The delegation from Tobeningo country is equally important, isn't it?"

They all laughed, as she continued, "Anyway, I thought you would ask me a much serious question, such as what I would have done had my identity been detected?

"And what would you have done?"

"Ah, son, I am supposed to keep feeding you even at your age? To answer your question, let's just say your mother cannot think, now. Can we just go home?"

Ganchu felt elated he was going to meet his father, after all. He looked over and saw his mother and Emerald in a cordial moment, then, out of nowhere, his heart jumped. The calm before the thunderstorm, he imagined, the moment he would tell this mother he had never really known - or the moment she would find out – that this woman was already mother to a grown up son, who was not his.

It was nearing daybreak as they entered the confines of Tobeningo. A sunbird flew right past them.

"What a daring bird, it almost plucked one's eye off!"

"I suppose that is why it was able to kill the elephant," Ganchu added, looking straight into his mother's eyes.

Everyone smiled.

Glossary

Ashawo: prostitute

Buy'am-sell'am: trader in (primarily) consumables

Dakifankwo: someone or thing, awkward and not particularly valued.

Garri-boy: ruffian; an irresponsible individual

Kabba: large, overflowing gown worn by women on casual occasions

Kenja: raffia-woven basket for carrying cargo on the head

Kwacha: drink prepared from fermented corn

Mimbo: general term for palm wine, corn-derived and other liquor

Mukala: white; Whiteman; colonial authority/government

Mungang: one who interacts with the spirit-world; medicine-man; magical powers

Obasinjom: the intermediary between the human and spirit worlds - equally dreaded and revered

Sanja: loin-wrap worn by menfolk

Segele: special solo dance performed to bring drummers and a dance to a halt.